Foul Ball

HAVEN HADLEY

Earned Run
Copyright ©2021 Haven Hadley

Cover Design by Haven Hadley
Photography by ©6:12 Photography by Eric McKinney
Editing by Barren Acres Editing
Proofreading by Landers Editorial Services

Declan

You've been traded to the Emperors.

Not exactly the phone call I expected to get two months into the season. Yet, here I stood in the middle of my living room trying to figure what in the hell to take with me for the trip up to Espen the day after tomorrow.

Three years in Maryland and I'd built a life here. Now, I had to pack it all up and go live in a hotel until I could find a house there and sell my place here. I knew the realities of being traded when I signed my contract with the Backfins. I just never expected it to be during the season. I guess I always thought if I was going to be traded it would happen between seasons and I'd have the opportunity to get settled before the new one started. Or at least get my shit together before I had to race off to a new city.

As of now, I had three days to get my ass to Espen and be on the field Friday night to play. I didn't have a fucking clue where to start.

The only benefit would be playing with Ayden Thompson again. The pitcher for my college team, Ayden, had left the year before I graduated and was now one of the starting pitchers for the Emperors.

Deciding to ignore everything else for now, I picked up my phone to call Ayden. If I was going to a new city, I wanted to look on the bright side of things. According to my agent, news of the trade wouldn't break until later in the evening while the Backfins and Emperors worked out the final details. Barring any drastic changes in their plans, I'd be in Espen by week's end.

The least I could do was give my friend a heads-up that I was coming his way. I sat in my favorite chair and groaned. The brown leather was buttery soft. No way would I stay in a hotel any longer than necessary and the chair was the first thing I'd move. Especially because staying in a hotel would fuck with my game.

Maybe I could crash with Ayden for a bit while I searched for a new place to live. Anything would be better than a hotel, even a suite. They were bad enough on the road, but to permanently live out of one would suck.

I hit send on the call and waited for him to answer.

"Hello?" There was an excited edge to his tone.

"Hey, Ayden, I heard something today—"

He cut me off before I could even finish my sentence. "How did you hear already?"

His question didn't make an ounce of sense. "Of course I would know. How did you find out before I did?"

"Well, because it was my wedding and since it was only Rome and me there, I'm pretty sure we were the first to know."

Wedding?

His words and excitement filtered past my own problems and everything clicked into place.

"Holy shit. You and Rome got married? How did I not know this? Congratulations!"

"Thanks. He surprised me while we were playing in Vegas. Once he proposed, we figured why wait."

I couldn't believe they got married and not a single gossip page had mentioned it. "Damn. You guys did a great job of keeping that under wraps."

Ayden laughed. "That's what happens when you slip the chapel owners extra money to keep things quiet until we goet back to Espen. I'm sure it will be all over the media sometime tomorrow after our flight arrives." I could hear the eye roll in his tone. "But if you didn't call about the wedding, what did you think I already knew?"

"Want to have dinner on Friday after the game?"

"We play the Redwoods on Friday not—" I waited for it to click into place. "Wait... Are you coming to Espen?"

"I got the call this morning. My first game is on Friday."

"Fuck me. Seriously?" There was a scratchiness on the line and Ayden's voice grew muffled. "No, Rome. It's Declan. He got traded to the Emperors." The line became clear again. "Damn, I can't believe you're joining us. We're going to kill it this season."

"It won't hit the news until tonight, but I take it you aren't going to miss Martin?"

Ayden sighed. "Don't get me wrong, Martin is a great guy, but he doesn't have the same level of play that he's had in the past. His bat isn't there anymore, neither is his speed. If we're gonna come back and win the Series this year, we need both, and you have them."

"Glad you think I do. It'll be nice to play with you again, but I'm not looking forward to living in a hotel until I can find a new place. Or dealing with selling my house."

"Yeah, that fucking sucks. You could stay with us while you look. I'm sure Rome wouldn't mind."

"Fine with me!" I heard Rome call out in the background.

While the offer was tempting, I knew I couldn't intrude on the newlyweds. With the season in full swing, they wouldn't have much time together. Too many road games left. "Nah, that's okay, but thanks for the offer. I'm gonna call Ethan and have him start looking online for me."

Ayden chuckled. "You know your brother is going to give you a load of shit for making him your real estate agent."

"Probably." I rolled my eyes thinking about his reaction. "Then his overbearing ass will agree to do it only so he can drive down and inspect every possible house and neighborhood I'm interested in."

"True. At least you know he'll pick a good place. If you change your mind before then, let me know."

"I will. I'm going to call Ethan. I'll see you on Friday."

"Looking forward to it."

I hung up with Ayden and immediately dialed my brother. Most likely he was at work. Unless he was on assignment, he should be sitting at his desk. Hopefully. The sooner I got this started, the sooner I could have a place with my own space in it.

I glanced around the room at the paintings and pictures on the walls. Thank fuck I could pay someone to pack all this shit and move it for me. It was nothing I felt like dealing with.

The phone connected and Ethan didn't waste time with small talk. "Hey, Declan. Why aren't you at the stadium getting ready for tonight's game?"

"Well, funny you should ask. That's why I'm calling."

"What, did you get hurt?" My brother immediately went into protective mode. With a six-year gap between us, Ethan had always been my biggest cheerleader but also my biggest protector. Sometimes to the point that it became overwhelming. "Do I need to drive down there? I can be there in about four hours. I'll grab Mom on the way." The sound of his keys rattling hit my ears. My brother may be overprotective, but he only wanted what was best for me.

"Relax, Ethan. I'm not hurt. I'm just not playing tonight because I'm no longer a Backfin."

The squeak of his chair told me he'd sat down again. "Did they trade you? Where are you going?" He was trying to be calm, except he wasn't good at covering the concern in his voice, no doubt worried I'd be shipped across the country.

"A little closer to home. They traded me to the Emperors. I play my first game there on Friday."

A crash filtered through the phone. Knowing my brother, it was most likely his chair falling to the ground when he jumped out of it. The entire freaking police station was now probably paying attention to my brother's antics. "That's fucking fantastic. I'll be able to bring Mom and Dad to more of your home games since you'll be much closer."

"Definitely one benefit. I'd love for you guys to be able to make it to more of them."

"So what's the plan? Do they help you move? What happens now?" He rambled a mile a minute.

I chuckled. "Are you going to give me a chance to answer before you keep asking questions?"

"Sorry. I'm just really excited about how much closer you'll be to home."

It actually surprised me when I'd signed with the Backfins that Ethan hadn't moved to Maryland to keep an eye on me. There was overprotective and there was going too far. That would have crossed the line into get the fuck out of my life. I loved my brother, but I also liked having my own space. Something I learned when I left for college.

As a kid, I'd worshipped the ground my brother walked on and would have done anything to get him and his friends' attention. In college, that all changed. I found myself there and, instead of looking up to my brother, I finally started to see him as my equal, which only helped to strengthen our relationship. He still thought he had to watch over me at times, but I knew it was only done out of love.

"I'm excited, too. Well, kind of. Not looking forward to selling my house and moving my shit. And I'm really not looking forward to staying in a hotel until I can find a place of my own."

"A hotel? Why would you need to stay in a hotel?"

I rested my ankle on top of my opposite knee and leaned back into the soft cushion. "The team isn't going to pay my rent and find me a place to live, but they will fork out the money for a suite for a few weeks while I get something."

"I didn't mean why wasn't the team finding a place, but why don't you stay with Brock?"

I hadn't even thought about the possibility of staying with him. Somehow, it hadn't crossed my mind when they told me I'd be going to the Emperors that I'd be living in the same city as him.

Brock Richmond.

My brother's best friend since they were kids, Brock had been a lineman for the Espen Sandpipers until he retired after the last season. I didn't know how to tell my brother it wasn't a good idea without him wanting to know the reason. A reason I had kept to myself from the time I was a teenager.

"I don't want to be in his way during retirement. Baseball is a lot of in and out the door, you know that." That seemed like the most neutral answer I could give. I didn't think my brother was ready for the truth yet.

Brock was my first crush on a guy. The first guy to help me realize I was bisexual.

I'd told my brother and parents long ago that I was attracted to both men and women, I just never mentioned to Ethan about my crush on Brock. All through high school, Brock and my brother played football together. Brock made a career out of it. My brother, on the other hand, wanted to become a cop. They both went their own ways, never losing a moment of their friendship.

During the college football season, Ethan would get tickets to the Espen University games, where Brock played, so we could drive down on a Saturday and watch. That was when I really started to notice the way I felt being around Brock. The attraction I had to him. Every week that there was a home game, we were there in the stands. And every week, even though I knew he was straight, I'd hope Brock would notice me.

It was a long time ago.

Since then, I'd come into my own, dating both men and women throughout college. During my first year in the majors, I kept my bi side hidden, then Callen came out and I didn't need to conceal it anymore. Not that there had been many men. My last friend with benefits was with a woman, which ended before I left for spring training back in February.

I hadn't seen Brock in person in years, but for some reason, I still compared every man to him.

"Brock won't care at all. I'll call him now."

Before I could protest, Ethan disconnected the call.

"Shit."

There was no way I could stop him now. The only thing I could hope was that Brock would say no to having Ethan's little brother as a roommate.

I didn't think I was that lucky, which meant instead of worrying about packing my stuff and moving in three days, I now had to worry about coming face-to-face with Brock Richmond.

Chapter 2

Brock

Mid-May in New Jersey. The weather was finally moving from the cold of winter to the warmth of spring. Though, sometimes we didn't get a long spring here. We'd go from needing heat to warm us to cranking on the air-conditioning. Today was perfect with the temperature hovering around seventy.

With my feet propped up on the deck railing, I tipped my head back and closed my eyes, letting the sun soak into my skin. The waves gently rolling to the shore soothed my soul. There was nothing better than this.

My years with the NFL paid off. I was able to purchase a home in full for my parents, pay for college for my brother, and buy this house for myself. I could have had a much bigger place, but that wasn't me. I was practical with my money. I saved and invested. Yes, the house was more than I needed, but it wasn't to the point of being ostentatious. Plus, it wasn't like I needed something overly secure. No one cared about a retired lineman.

As if reminding me I wasn't alone, Sampson, my five-year-old Akita, came over and put his head on my arm. He was almost completely black with white markings on his chest and the tip of his tail. At a hundred and ten pounds, he was a big dog and all the security I needed, in addition to the system on my house, which my best friend, Ethan, was adamant I put in.

Now, if only I could get the courage to start dating. It was something I hadn't done in all my years playing professionally. Women would throw themselves at me, even when the Sandpipers were playing terribly. But it wasn't a woman I wanted. I lied and told anyone who asked I was focused on playing and didn't have time to date.

Only two people knew my secret. I didn't need to hide my sexuality anymore now that I was retired, yet I still did. I always worried if everyone found out I was gay, while I was still active, I could lose my spot on the team. Or I'd alienate my teammates. I couldn't do anything to jeopardize the income I had coming in.

If only I had the balls to get out there and search for what I wanted. A romantic connection. A man who only had eyes for me. Someone I could build a life with. I wasn't looking for hookups. I was too old for that, and I'd done those in the past when I was covered with a disguise so no one saw the real me. Now I wanted something with substance.

My phone rang, pulling me from my thoughts. Sampson laid down by my chair, his gaze out toward the ocean. I glanced to where my phone sat on the small table on my other side and noticed my best friend's name flash on the screen. A smile immediately lit my face.

"Superstar, how's it going?" I greeted.

Ethan chuckled. "I wish you would knock that off. Solving a high-profile case doesn't make me a superstar."

"It does when it becomes national news."

"That was a year ago, Brock."

"You'll always be a superstar to me." If he would have been in front of me, I'd have winked.

I loved busting on Ethan. He did, in fact, solve a case that had been cold for far too long. It made it onto all the major networks. But Ethan had said time and time again he was just doing his job. And now it was mine to remind him, as often as I could, just how amazing he was, even if it meant me doing it with a little bit of humor.

Ethan sighed.

I laughed. This was too much fun. "You mean you didn't call so I could remind you of your accolades?"

"Not even close. I know you have contacts in Espen. Did you hear about Declan?"

"No, what's going on?" Ethan liked to tell me about his brother. He didn't know I kept up with Declan and watched his games on TV when I could. Now that I was retired, it was often. And Declan was a hell of a player.

"I'm sure it will be out later today, but he's been traded to Espen. He plays his first game with them on Friday."

"Get out. Declan's coming here?"

"Yeah, and he needs a place to stay. That's why I'm calling you."

"He can stay with me for as long as he needs to." There was no hesitation on my part. I'd do anything for the Armitage family. Growing up, they were like a second home to me. They would feed me dinner and pack up enough leftovers to feed my parents and brother. Without having much to our names, every bit helped.

I could hear the smile in his voice. "I knew you'd say that. I'll call Declan and let him know."

"I have no plans, so I'll be here whenever he arrives. Make sure you give him my number in case he has any problems."

"Will do. And, Brock?"

"Yeah, man?"

"Hands off."

I nearly dropped the phone in shock. Yes, Ethan was overly protective of Declan, but not once had I made a single comment about being interested in him sexually. "Excuse me?"

"You're gay, he's bi. Nothing more than friends between you two."

"Are you serious right now? Just because we both like men doesn't mean we'll fall into bed together. I've never even looked at him that way."

"Good, keep it like that. Promise me, Brock."

"If you were in front of me, I'd hit you for saying that. I shouldn't have to promise you anything, but because I've known you most of my life, I know how serious you take your promises. So I promise. Hands off. And before you say anything else, bring this up again and I am going

16

to hit you the next time I see you. I'm your best friend. If you can't trust me, I worry about the rest of your relationships."

"Yeah, yeah, you know how I feel about my brother."

"I do, but he's an MLB player. Loosen up a bit. Besides, he doesn't even know I'm gay." I'd be lying if I didn't recognize how much his words hurt. He must have heard it in my tone.

"I'm sorry."

"Whatever. Just give him my number." I was about to hang up, irritated by the whole conversation, when Ethan's voice cut through.

"Brock?"

"It's fine."

"You know I love you."

"Too bad you don't swing my way."

"Even if I did, we'd be at each other's throats."

I chuckled, feeling myself relax. "We would." Also, the only time I found him attractive was when I was seventeen and my hormones were going crazy. I got over it fast when I walked in on him making out with Missy Reynolds. The whole scene was a huge turnoff and cured me of seeing Ethan that way.

"I gotta go. Thanks for doing this for Declan and me."

"Anytime."

We hung up and I tipped my head back, trying to find the peace I felt before the phone call. It wouldn't come. Instead, I stood and went into the house through the sliding door with Sampson on my heels. He quickly jumped up to rest on the couch while I glanced around the room.

Light gray hardwood floors with a dark gray U-shaped sectional and white walls, my living room was light and airy. This level had an open concept, flowing from one room to the next. The kitchen was pristine with white cabinets, pale blue granite counters, and stainless-steel appliances. There were so many windows in the house, I couldn't go far without a gorgeous, oceanfront view.

I guess I didn't need to clean down here in preparation for Declan to arrive. That was what happened when I retired and suddenly had a lot of time on my hands. My house was spotless. The upstairs was as well.

Reaching into the refrigerator, I pulled out a couple of chicken breasts and heated up a pan. It was hard to adjust from eating as much as I did when I was playing to what I needed to eat now. I still exercised regularly. I had an entire room dedicated to staying in shape.

When I was on the field, I came in at just over three hundred pounds. I was an offensive lineman. It was like I was born into that position with how quickly and broadly I grew. At two-seventy presently, I'd lost some weight since I'd been home. It wasn't easy, though. I ate a lot to stay in the size and shape I needed to be. Now it was a matter of getting some more of that weight off and not consuming so many calories.

I'd never be one of those guys who was ripped with muscles and ready to show them off, but I was muscular at this weight. I had to be. No six-pack on me nor did I have a big gut. My stomach was flat, just not defined. I'd probably look ridiculous if I lost too much weight. I needed to find my perfect spot.

Sampson picked his head up to look at me once the scent of seasoned chicken floated throughout the space.

"No way, buddy. You're not getting any of this."

He huffed out a breath before dropping his head back down.

When lunch was done and arranged on the plate with a generous helping of rice and a salad, I took it over to the four-person dining table I had in the corner of the room. As I ate, I watched the ocean. There weren't a lot of people out there yet, nothing like it would be when they came from out of town every weekend in the summer.

For months it had been Sampson and me. I had friends who'd stop by and visit. Lali was here more than anyone else. She was the PR person for the Sandpipers and had become someone I was very close to. Not quite as close as Ethan but almost. And Lali was the only other person besides him who knew I was gay.

Maybe it would be good having Declan here. I'd have someone else to cook for, which I loved to do. Sure, he'd be busy playing and he'd be on the road often, but it would still be better than being alone all the time.

We could hang out. I could show him around Espen on his days off. If he wanted that, which I wasn't sure he would. He was young and in his prime, while I was older and not that fun. It wasn't that I didn't want to be, I just was never the party type of person. There were also days when my body didn't like cooperating and moving around was difficult. Those years of playing football finally caught up to me.

"You ready to have a roommate?" I asked Sampson. He wasn't a great conversationalist, but I loved him more than I did most people.

He shifted his eyes in my direction then went back to looking out the sliding door.

When I used to travel for games, Lali took care of him for me. She had a great condo in the city that didn't mind pets. Sampson seemed to think he was on vacation every time he was there. He'd be more energetic and ready to go.

A text came through on my phone where it sat next to my glass on the table.

Unknown: Hey, Brock, it's Declan. Thanks for letting me stay with you. I promise not to be in the way.

I saved his contact information and replied.

Me: You couldn't be in the way here. Let me know when you're packed and driving up.

I sent him my address. I already had a spare key in the drawer and one of my two garage bays was empty since I only had my Toyota Sequoia. Flashy I was not.

Declan: I'll put a lot of my stuff in storage, so I won't take up too much of your space.

Me: Dec, honestly, bring whatever you want. I'll make room. Also, I'm not sure if Ethan mentioned it, but I hope you like dogs. Sampson is part of the package deal when you stay here.

Declan: I love dogs. Thanks again, Brock. I'll see you soon.

I wasn't sure how long Declan would be staying with me, but while he did, I wanted him to feel like this was his home.

Ethan's words rattled around my mind again. *Hands off.* I shook my head. I wasn't interested in Declan, nor had I ever been. This was simply a friend helping a friend. Or rather, family helping family. I'd always be here for them.

Chapter 3

Declan

"Turn right in point two miles."

At least the GPS knew where the hell we were going. The only times I'd been to Espen were when my brother drove us directly to the university stadium, when Ethan and I went to Sandpipers games, or when the team took us to the hotel. Shuttles took us to the games and I only left the hotel to have dinner with Ayden. *Thank fuck for Uber,* I thought as I glanced around the massive city.

Espen had to be the biggest MLB city on the East Coast. Probably twice the size of some of the others. It might take me a bit, but I'd figure out my way around. I glanced in my rearview mirror and remembered I couldn't see shit through the back window. I'd packed up what I needed for now—clothes and toiletries. Everything else could wait until I found a place of my own. The movers would be at my house next week to pack the rest of my stuff and take it to storage, then the real estate agent would be by to put the place up for sale.

I was glad I didn't have to wait for that to happen to find somewhere of my own. I'd probably rent until the house sold, then find something I really loved in Espen. Ayden had a beautiful house right outside of the city, which made me wonder what kind of place Brock had when he lived within the city limits. The only thing I would miss would be my Mercedes AMG. Beautiful car, no trunk space.

The rental was due back tomorrow. I'd already looked at the schedule for my next day off so I could drive down and pick up my car. Luckily, the city had lots of options to get from one place to another until then.

"Turn right." I followed the GPS instructions, trying to figure out where it might be taking me. "Your destination is ahead on the left." Inching forward, I saw the number of the house and almost didn't believe it. "You have arrived." Apparently, I was in the right place. I just had no idea that Brock's house was on the beach. Fuck, what a way to live.

I pulled up to the curb and turned off the engine as reality hit me in the face. Parked in front of Brock's beach house, there was no escaping the fact that I agreed to live with my brother's best friend. The guy I had a crush on as a teenager. I needed to remember I was older and wiser than the kid who wanted to follow my big brother and his bestie around.

No, I wasn't that kid anymore.

I was a Major League Baseball player and right fielder for the Espen Emperors. I didn't need to crush on my older brother's straight best friend. Over and over again, I chanted that in my head as I climbed from the car.

Poor Brock probably didn't need me interfering in his peace, but I also knew he wouldn't turn my brother down when he asked. He was too nice to say no.

There was a two-car garage with a door next to it, which I guessed only led into the garage. To the left, I saw a staircase connected to a porch and another door. Which looked more like the entrance to the house. I climbed the stairs and lifted my hand to ring the bell when the door swung open.

"Declan!" Brock was smiling wide.

Fuck, he looked good. Better than I remembered. He'd lost weight since playing football. That had to be a given, though. No need to keep on the weight of a lineman when you weren't playing. Dark, nearly black scruff surrounded his mouth that matched the color on his head. That kind of facial hair could give a nice beard burn.

Stop it, Declan.

Jesus, I couldn't be in the guy's presence for less than a minute before I started lusting after him. This was not going to go well.

"Hi, Brock. I'm sorry Ethan put you up to this, but I appreciate you letting me stay with you. I promise to be out of your hair as soon as possible."

He stepped back. "Don't worry. I actually offered for you to stay when he mentioned you were traded. Come on in. It'll be nice to have someone else here besides Sampson." At the mention of his name, a large black dog with a few spots of white came around the corner, his tongue hanging out as he panted.

Growing up with dogs, I dropped my hand, letting him smell me. His cold nose touched my fingers as he decided whether he liked me or not. After a moment, he moved to my side. I squatted down, petting his head. "Aren't you friendly."

"Declan, this is Sampson." Brock turned to the dog. "What do you think, buddy? Want Declan to stay with us for a little while?"

Sampson took that moment to swipe his tongue up my cheek. I laughed. "I'll take that as a yes."

"He may never let you leave. Let me show you around and then we can grab your stuff from the car."

"Works for me." I gave Sampson one last pat on the head, then stood to follow Brock. My eyes wandered to his ass and I pinched my leg. I was not going to lust after a straight man. There were plenty of single men and women in Espen.

Too bad I didn't know anyone as well as Jessica. The friends with benefits gig we had going worked. At least until she started seeing some guy right before spring training. It all worked out in the end. We were still friends and her boyfriend was a great guy. Now, with me hours away in Espen, that arrangement would have fallen apart anyway.

It was a nice reality check. The time for me to stop sleeping around had come. Dating and settling down started to sound better and better each day. Maybe Espen was the place I'd find the person to make that happen with.

"Kitchen and living room," Brock said, gesturing to the space. The room was open, the light from the multitude of windows brightening the room. "There's a gaming console under the TV. Not that I think you'll have a lot of time to play, considering your new schedule."

"Tell me about it. At least the Emperors got back from a long road run last night."

Brock pointed down a hall to the left. "There's a weight room down there. All the bedrooms are on the second floor."

I followed him up the stairs where he showed me his room and the two guest rooms, pointing out the one I'd be staying in. "This is great. I still feel bad intruding."

Brock shook his head. "Don't. I told you I offered when Ethan called."

I'd been so focused on the sexy man in front of me, then his dog, that I'd missed when he said that. "You did, but I don't get why."

"We're family. I'll do anything to help out when you need it. Now, let's grab your stuff and get you settled. Then we can have lunch."

We went back downstairs and out to the car, carrying bag after bag inside. It only took a couple trips to get everything into the house.

"That's the last one." I slammed the trunk closed and locked the car.

"You don't have to leave your car out here. I have an empty bay in the garage."

"Nah, it's just a rental. They're going to come pick it up tomorrow morning." I started back toward the front door.

"Where's your car?" Brock shut the door behind us and went straight to the kitchen.

I took the bottle of water he handed me. "In Maryland. I have a Mercedes AMG. Not exactly the moving kind of car. I'll need to drive down one of these days to grab it. I left it locked up tight in my garage."

Brock opened a cabinet and pulled out a pan. "I can drive you down to get it. If you don't want to wait for a day off, I'm up early. We can go and be back before you'd need to be at the stadium."

"You don't have to do that."

"I don't mind." He grabbed a pack of chicken out of the fridge. "Hungry? Chicken Caesar salad?"

"Starving, but you don't have to cook for me. We can order something." I started to feel bad. Brock wanted to help at every turn, but I didn't want to seem like I was taking advantage.

"I really enjoy cooking. It'll be nice to cook for more than one person. Sampson doesn't get people food." He pointed to the chairs at the counter. "Sit and relax."

"I can't leave you cooking while I watch. I can help."

"I'm good, but you can do the dishes when we're done. Not my favorite." He laughed and placed the chicken in the smoking pan.

"Deal." I sat down and took a sip of the water. At least with washing the dishes I was doing something to contribute.

It shouldn't have surprised me that Brock wanted to do whatever he could to be kind and helpful. It had been the same thing when I was growing up. Anytime he could help my mom or dad with something, he did. When it came to my math homework, it was always Brock who showed me how to find the answer. Ethan's strengths laid with my history assignments.

"What do you think about being traded?" He glanced over his shoulder while he flipped the chicken.

I shrugged. "Not sure. I know the Emperors gave up more to get me, and I'm excited to play with Ayden again. But then I think about the friendships I made on the Backfins. It kinda sucks to leave everything I've known since graduating college."

Brock set a head of lettuce on the cutting board on the counter and started chopping it. "Yeah, but you don't have to lose those friendships. Players get traded more often in the NFL. I've had plenty of friends come and go from the Sandpipers. We still see each other at events, though."

"I know we'll keep in touch, but I'll miss the day-to-day. Then trying to find a new place to live. I figure I'll rent until my house sells, then I'll buy something here."

He stopped what he was doing and looked up. "You don't have to rent. You are more than welcome to stay until you sell the house."

My eyes were drawn to the way he gripped the knife and I wanted to smack myself upside the head. Right there was the perfect reason why staying with Brock too long was a bad idea. Apparently, my crush may have died with my teenage years, that didn't mean the lust I'd felt for Brock had. Dear god, I had to find a way to keep my dick in check around him.

"We'll see." I couldn't bring myself to say *hell no* and hurt Brock's feeling.

Somehow, someway, I needed to get a grip on myself. It wasn't like I just figured out my bi side. Hell, until high school when I made out with one of the cheerleaders behind the bleachers, I'd wondered if I was gay. I'd known for a long time that I liked both men and women. So why was this one man sending my system haywire? And why the hell did it need to be a straight man who turned me on to the point of not being able to use my brain properly?

Brock finished up the salads and set a plate in front of me. This was not a homemade salad. It looked as if it came from a restaurant.

"Shit, this looks amazing. Way better than anything I could have ever ordered." I picked up my fork and dug in.

Brock took the seat next to me, starting in on his own salad. As we ate, I realized I'd only talked about myself up until that point. I hadn't seen Brock in years. The least I could do was learn what he'd been up to. I knew he'd played with the Sandpipers. Hell, for his first two years, my brother and I went to the home games. Once I'd gone to college, I wasn't living here for most of the year anymore.

"What made you decide to retire?"

Chapter 4

Brock

What did I get myself into? Seeing Declan on TV was nothing compared to seeing him in person. The TV didn't do him justice. Or maybe it was his uniform. Because looking at him now in a pair of shorts and a T-shirt that clung to his muscles, he was gorgeous. He wasn't a huge guy, but it was clear he worked out with how defined he was. At least, from what I could see. My imagination ran rampant with what he looked like underneath his clothes, which I did not need to be thinking about.

And when he smiled, those dimples appeared and about did me in. I forgot about them. Having never looked at Declan in any way other than my best friend's kid brother, this was a huge shock to my system. One I couldn't afford to have. Especially when I promised Ethan I'd keep my hands off him. Who knew seeing Declan Armitage would be a test of my willpower?

Nope. Not going there. Declan was no one I could have anything with. I certainly couldn't get hard at the sight of him.

After our lunch together, I went out the sliding door and onto the deck. I needed to clear my head and get the smell of Declan out of my lungs. Whatever he used, whether it was aftershave or his shampoo, I wasn't sure, but it was not helping me keep my libido in check.

Sampson came with me and decided to lie closer to the railing so his nose stuck through the bottom of it. When it got hotter in the peak of summer, I'd keep him in the house more. He had a double coat and preferred the air-conditioning over the blazing sun. Even with the breeze from the ocean, it wasn't enough to keep him cool outside.

I should have grabbed a book to bring with me, but I didn't think of anything except getting away from Declan after we ate and caught up with one another. The other spare bedroom in my house had a wall of bookshelves. Reading was one of my favorite things to do to relax. There was no better backdrop for a good book than the salty sea air and the sound of the waves.

The sliding door opened behind me and closed.

"Damn, it's beautiful here," Declan said as he walked over and leaned against the railing. He closed his eyes and breathed the fresh air in. Sampson picked up his head to get a better look at him. He was going to have to get used to having someone else in his space.

"It's one of the reasons I bought it. Life was always so hectic when I was playing. I needed an escape off the field."

When Declan asked me earlier why I retired, I mostly told him the truth. That I was tired. My body was hurting. My heart wasn't in it. I left off that I was sick of hiding who I was and being alone.

I could have come out and stayed on the team longer. I knew having Tim Deary and Kasper Warnes-Wilder as the new owners, I wouldn't be ousted for being gay. Not that I thought I would under the old owner. But it wasn't just them. It was the fans and my teammates. The reporters who would be in my face during interviews, asking me questions, who didn't have any business doing so. Yes, being a professional player invited people into my personal life, but I hated that. It was easier hiding that part of myself and staying out of the spotlight while I was still on the team.

"Do you go in the ocean a lot?" Declan asked, pulling me from my thoughts.

"Usually in the evenings when there are fewer people on the beach. I don't exactly have a great body to show off." I didn't hate how I looked, but I'd always been self-conscious since I was a bigger guy. It wasn't like I could go out on the sand and peel my shirt off to watch people drool over me. Not that I'd want attention on me like that anyway.

Declan turned to face me, leaning against the railing. "Are you kidding? You look great." And now I was blushing. Lovely.

I smoothed my hand down my shirt. No hard ridges of muscles to be felt on my stomach. I shrugged.

He sat down in the chair beside mine. "Seriously, Brock. If you go down there, you're going to have women all over you."

I had to bite my tongue from revealing it wasn't women I wanted looking at me. For some reason, I wasn't ready to tell Declan about that part of myself yet. Maybe it was because, once I did, I was afraid he'd be angry I never told him before. I didn't lie when I said I considered him family. And family wasn't supposed to hide things from each other. Yet, I did.

He wouldn't be the only one I'd have to tell. I didn't want my parents or my brother, Wyatt, to find out through the media. It wouldn't be right.

The relationship I had with my family was strong. Growing up in a tiny apartment, we didn't have much. What we did have in spades was love. My mom and dad did the best they could to teach Wyatt and me that money wasn't everything. That we could still have a good life without it. They were right, but that didn't mean money didn't help. It was why, as soon as I could, I got them out of that apartment and into a house where they wouldn't have a mortgage. It wasn't a huge place; my parents would never accept that. But it was a nice house. They both took extra special care of it.

Turning, I noticed Declan looking at me. He grinned. "What's got you so lost in your head?"

"Just thinking about my parents. It's been a few months since I've seen them in person." Which was ridiculous. I had all the time in the world now but didn't feel like driving to visit. That needed to change, especially with Wyatt graduating college next week.

"How are they doing?"

"Good." I smiled. I couldn't help it. I might not see them often, but we talked on the phone at least once a week, sometimes on video. I also got on video chat with

Wyatt often. "Mom is still working at the daycare center. Dad has a job with a landscaper."

"And Wyatt?"

I loved talking about my brother. He was ten years younger than me. My parents didn't plan on having any more kids after me, since they were struggling as it was with money, but then Mom got pregnant with Wyatt. I remember being so excited when he was born. Even though I was older than him, I was always there when he needed me.

"He's doing good. He graduates next week with his bachelor's in social work."

"That's great. And you got your bachelor's in psychology, right?"

I nodded. "Yeah."

"You two could team up and do something together. I bet you want to relax for a bit first, though." It wasn't a bad idea. One I hadn't thought about before. I wasn't sure what Wyatt's plans were after he graduated. He said he wanted to take the summer off before diving into the workforce. I couldn't blame him.

Wyatt wasn't the type who went to college and partied. He was a lot like me that way. He didn't take for granted that I paid for his education. Day and night my brother worked his ass off and his grades reflected it.

For me, a couple times since I retired, I thought about going back to school and getting my master's. When I was still in college, I was scouted and knew my family could use the money football would provide. My education was put on hold once I got my bachelor's degree. But I wouldn't compromise that. I was determined to graduate with my degree before going to the NFL.

I didn't regret the decisions I made. My family was set now. No need for them to worry about keeping a roof over their heads. I had enough money saved where I never had to work again if I didn't want to. I couldn't sit around the house forever, though. I'd be bored out of my mind.

"There you go getting lost in your head again," Declan observed.

I chuckled. "Sorry. I'm not used to having someone around the house. All this free time on my hands allows my mind to wander."

"I won't stay too long. You'll get your peace and quiet back soon enough."

He went to stand but I reached over and clasped his forearm gently to stop him. "I like having you here. It's been too quiet. Sampson doesn't answer my questions when I talk to him." I smiled. "Really, Dec. Stay as long as you want. You're doing me a favor by keeping me company."

Declan nodded and eased back into the chair, mimicking me by putting his feet on the railing. "Why didn't you move closer to your parents after you were done playing?"

"It wasn't home to me any longer. I love it here. I couldn't give this up." I jutted my chin toward the ocean. "And while I love my parents dearly, I don't need them hovering over me. Even though I'm thirty-two, my mom would smother me."

A laugh bubbled up out of Declan and damn it sounded good. "I remember the times your family would come over for Thanksgiving. Your mom hugged me within an inch of my life."

I smiled again. Those were great visits. Once Ethan and I solidified our best friend status, his parents invited mine over for Thanksgiving. It became a tradition. My mom would bring a couple side dishes then help Ethan's dad in the kitchen. Ethan and I would go outside with my dad and throw the football around. Declan would join in sometimes and we'd form teams. Wyatt did when he was older, but we were always careful around him, not wanting to run him over since he was smaller and younger than all of us.

Those traditions stopped sometime during college. It was more challenging getting everyone together. Our families would always be intertwined in one way or another.

Declan rubbed his hand over his stomach. "Now I want turkey."

I laughed. "We're still months away from November."

I was so wrapped up in memories and conversation with Declan, I didn't hear someone come into my home. The sliding door opening caused me to jump from my chair and turn. Sampson got up when I did, but he wasn't angry at who came outside. No, he went over to her with his tail wagging to love up on her when she bent down.

Lali had her long, platinum blonde hair up in a messy bun. Her tank top showed off her two full sleeves of colorful tattoos. Ripped jeans showed more ink on her left thigh.

"Who's my good boy?" she cooed to Sampson. Some days I swore he loved her more than me.

Lali lifted her head to smile at me then her eyes immediately went to Declan. She stood and held out her hand. "Lali Romano. You must be Declan." I had mentioned to her about him staying with me.

He stood and shook her hand. "I am. It's nice to meet you." Then he turned to me. "You didn't tell me you were dating anyone." This happened often with Lali and me. Every time we were together, people who didn't know us thought we were a couple.

Lali busted out laughing. "Um, no. I love Brock like a brother." She turned to me. "No offense." She'd never out me. While we did treat each other like siblings at times, there was zero romantic connection between us. Though the way she was eyeing up Declan had the hair on the back of my neck standing up.

Instead of saying anything, I nudged her with my foot to break her Declan-induced trance. I understood it. He was gorgeous.

Her eyes narrowed when she glanced my way before she broke into a big grin. Damn, was I that transparent? I hoped not. Declan didn't need to know how attractive I found him. And honestly, it wouldn't be the worst thing if these two dated. But why did the idea of that bother me so much?

"Lali is my close friend and she's also the PR person for the Sandpipers," I stated.

"That's me," she cut in. "Someone has to keep those men in line and not all over the tabloids."

"Is that how you two met?" Declan asked.

I nodded. "When she first got hired, she was so different from the guy who held the job before her. He walked around like he had a stick shoved up his ass. No one liked him. After him trying for months and months without success to get the players to work with him, he finally gave up and put in his notice. Our then owner, Kyle, brought Lali on. We all instantly fell in love with her energetic personality. Plus, she didn't take shit from anyone."

Lali put her arm around my waist. I was a solid ten inches taller than her five-foot-seven-inch frame. "And I fell in love with this guy back." She patted me on the chest with her other hand. "Don't get me wrong, I get along with the players well, but Brock is special."

I slung my arm over her shoulders and pressed a kiss to the top of her head. It was strictly platonic. I was one of those people who liked to show affection. Always had been. I got it from my mom. It was tough not to reach out and hug Declan when he showed up, but we hadn't seen each other in person in so long, I wasn't sure how he'd take it.

"You'll be seeing her around while you're staying here," I told Declan. "She likes to spontaneously show up and try to steal my dog."

"It's not my fault he loves me more," she replied.

Declan crouched down to pet Sampson. "I have my work cut out for me if I'm going to be his favorite."

Lali laughed. "That you do."

As I looked at Declan, Lali, and Sampson, I felt my chest warm. I wasn't alone in my house with just my dog for company. Sure, Lali came by often, but having

Declan here added something more. This sense of family I'd been missing in my home.

It was selfish of me to hope Declan would stay here for a while and not rush to buy something once his house sold. It was also incredibly foolish since I shouldn't be having thoughts about the man, except for him being Ethan's brother. Yet, when I looked at him smiling while Sampson licked his chin, I couldn't help but think how right it felt to have him here.

Declan

The air felt different as I walked into the Emperors' stadium. Weird since it wasn't the first time I played here. Being in the same division, the Emperors and the Backfins played each other a couple times during the season. I'd been to this stadium many times, just not headed toward the home team locker room.

Wooden lockers filled the area. Each player's uniform hanging there waiting for them. There was a door off to the left where I could see a light on under it. I figured it was Joe's office. I would knock in a second, after I gave myself a chance to acclimate to my new surroundings. Four years in Maryland and it felt a bit traitorous to be standing here.

I wandered through the rows of lockers, looking for my own, knowing it would already be set up with my stuff, delivered by the team from Maryland, and my new jersey. There on the left-hand side, I saw Armitage 33, but it looked off in the navy blue and yellow. Definitely something I would have to get used to.

I opened the drawers and saw my stuff had arrived safely. There would be time to organize it after I checked in with Joe. Hell, that had been the whole reason for coming to the field early. At least that was what I'd told myself. Deep down, I came early to get settled into the place. I knew it would take a little getting used to before this place felt like home.

Heading back the way I came, I knocked on the closed door. After a second, it opened and Joe appeared. His normal gruff demeanor in my presence shifted as he smiled at me. Probably for the first time in my career. Couldn't blame him, though. It was kind of hard to have good thoughts about a member of the opposing team during a game.

Joe reached his hand out to me immediately. "Declan, welcome to Espen."

"Thanks." I took his hand and shook.

"A little unsettling, isn't it?" He let go and I shoved my hands into my pockets.

Was I really that transparent? "Kinda. Not exactly what I expected for this year."

"Well, I'll tell ya, we're thrilled to have you. Been working on the GM over there in Maryland for at least the last six months. Knew we'd need your bat and defense if we were going to make it back to the Series this year and win."

Hearing those words from Joe's mouth released a bit of the tension in my gut. No one wanted to be the player who got pawned off on someone else because they weren't playing up to the standards of everyone else on the team.

"Wow, I didn't know the Emperors had been trying to trade for me."

Joe's brows drew together. "Are you telling me no one on the Backfins talked to you before the trade happened?"

I rocked back on my feet and glanced around, not exactly sure how to answer the question. "Can't say they did. The first time I heard anything about the trade was Wednesday morning when my agent called."

Joe shook his head. "That's some bullshit right there. You'll find here in Espen, we play it straight. If Tim or I are thinking about a trade, you'll know before we even talk to your agent. We don't play that behind closed doors bullshit."

"Have to say I really appreciate that. It'll be nice to not be blindsided if I ever get traded again."

"Well, let's hope that doesn't happen." He gestured down the row of lockers to where I'd found mine. "We got everything set up when it came in. Even had your number available." He glanced up at the clock on the wall. "I need to finish today's lineup, but give me ten minutes and I'll take you on a tour."

"That would be great. Or if you want, I'll make Ayden show me."

He chuckled. "I almost forgot you played with him in college."

"Yep, it'll be nice to be on the same team as him again. Just don't tell him that."

"Don't tell me what?" I glanced over my shoulder at the sound of Ayden's voice.

"Thompson, what are you doing here so early? You're not even on the mound today."

He shrugged and walked over, wrapping his arm around my shoulders. "Figured I'd make sure this guy gets the welcome he deserves."

Joe rolled his eyes. "I'd warn him about your normal bullshit, but since he's known you since college, I'm pretty sure he's already aware."

"Very aware," I chimed in, giving Joe my best innocent look. Joe had a much better relationship with the players here than my old manager did. Great guy, but he didn't bother with the shenanigans in the locker room.

"Somehow, I have a feeling you'll fit right in." Joe waved us off and walked back into his office, partially closing the door.

I looked at it then back to Ayden who laughed. "Joe knows better than to shut the door when Dominic comes in. If he knows Joe is listening, he's much better behaved."

I turned to Ayden and pulled him into a hug. "Congratulations, man. Super fucking happy for you."

He slapped me on the back. "Thanks. I didn't expect Rome to be so spontaneous, but I couldn't be happier." That was evident when he pulled back and his face was wreathed in an ear-to-ear smile. "So, what do you think about Espen so far? The hotel they put you up in okay?"

"Actually, I'm not in one."

"Then where are you staying? You didn't take me up on my offer. Did you find a place already?"

I wandered back down to my new locker and began organizing the stuff in the drawers. "No. Remember, I told you about Ethan's best friend? Brock Richmond?"

"Yeah, I remember." He took a seat in the chair next to mine. "Lineman for the Sandpipers. Didn't he retire this year?"

"He did. And he's got a house on the beach. Ethan asked him if I could stay there until I sold my house or bought a new one of my own."

"Figures," Ayden chuckled. "Still finding a way to keep an eye on you when you move."

"Probably." I decided not to mention the teenage crush on a straight guy that wanted to rear its ugly head. Hopefully, soon I'd be able to bury that shit back in the box it snuck out of.

"Come on, I'll give you the tour before everyone else gets here."

Ayden showed me around the Emperors' facilities. The place had everything we needed and in much better condition than Maryland. Tim Deary really took care of his team. The locker room was already bustling with players when we stepped back inside.

"Armitage!" I heard shouted across the room at me. "You ready to play with the big boys?"

"Fuck, Dominic," Ayden grumbled.

"Depends. Let me know when you find a big boy, then I'll tell you."

As we walked farther into the room and found Dominic Truby, the first baseman, standing in the middle of it grabbing his crotch. "Don't know about you, but I got a pretty big one here."

I frowned and shook my head, playing it up because Ayden had warned me about Dominic when I first met him. Great guy, loyal to a fault, and would give the shirt off his back to anyone who needed it, but he also loved to fuck around and laugh.

"Well, I guess if you consider only a handful big," I said in a mock innocent tone.

The room burst out laughing, while Dominic stared me down for a minute. He opened his mouth and I braced myself for whatever left his tongue next. What I hadn't expected was great gusty shouts of laughter. "Fuck, that was good." He held his hand out to me. "Welcome to Espen."

Still laughing, Dominic returned to his locker to get ready, and Ayden followed me over to mine. This time, he dropped in the chair across from me and I noticed the jersey with his name on it in the locker directly behind mine. I sat down in my chair and started tugging off my shirt when Callen Teague walked over.

"Glad you're here. Can't wait to see what you do on our side of the field."

Callen had to be the best shortstop in Major League Baseball. A once-in-a-lifetime player. That was when it really hit me where I was. I looked around at the different faces. While it was still strange, I finally started to understand why Ayden loved being in Espen so much. "Thanks. Excited to be here." It was the first time I said those words and truly meant them.

Another chair rolled over next to mine. "I think a drink is in order after the game."

I looked over to see Marcus sitting next to me. "Sounds good to me. I will say, I'll miss your smart-ass mouth while I'm batting."

Marcus shrugged, a smirk lifting the corner of his lips. "What can I say? I like ruffling feathers on the field."

"That you do." I smiled, knowing what an understatement that was. Marcus Warnes-Wilder was known for his smack talk behind the plate. Only second behind Wagner, the catcher for the Backfins.

"Come on, let's celebrate tonight. Nothing else to do anyway." Vander Devlin, the Emperors' left fielder pouted.

"Jesus Christ, Vander. Are you really going to mope because Evan is hanging out with his sister tonight?" Callen shook his head and reached for the hem of his own shirt.

Vander flipped him off. "You'd be bitchy too if you got home and Spencer wasn't there."

"Wrong. Remember, Spencer takes clients at night. Plenty of times he's not home when I get there. It's not my fault you two can't go a day without fucking like rabbits." I glanced back and forth between the two men.

"They're always like this," Ayden answered my unspoken question. "They'll kiss and make up in a few minutes."

"I'm not kissing him," they both said at the same time, which only brought more laughter into the locker room.

Marcus kicked Ayden's foot where he had it resting on a small table. "Don't instigate. The only reason you're paying a damn bit of attention to what's going on is because you're not playing tonight."

Ayden leaned his elbows on the armrest and steepled his fingers together. "True. But I still have to go get in my practice pitches."

"Still listen to music and ignore everyone else before a game?"

Marcus elbowed me in the side. "See, even Declan knows your bullshit."

"Not taking the bait. If something works, I'm sticking with it."

"I'm sure you're sticking a lot of things lately," Dominic said passing by, to which Ayden moved his foot causing Dominic to stumble.

Dominic whirled around and Ayden laughed with his hands up. "Hey, I thought we were acting like we were five. Just thought I'd play, too."

I didn't join in on any of the ribbing, besides my dig at Dominic, knowing the only person I had that level of relationship with was Ayden. I'd get to know everyone better and probably before long be right in the middle of all of it with everyone else.

Instead, I turned and took my jersey off the hanger and held it up for a second before pulling it on and starting in on the buttons. When I looked up again, Marcus was watching me.

"Weird, isn't it?"

"Weird?" I asked.

He gestured at where I finished with the last button. "Putting on a jersey you're not used to wearing."

"It really fucking is." I dropped back down into my chair. "Does it ever get not weird?"

"After a couple of games. But it'll take a few to get used to it all." Marcus tugged on his own jersey.

"I will say, it'll be nice to not get booed standing out in the field."

He stood and reached for his pants. "Ain't that the truth."

"Hurry up," Joe called. "We've got a game to play." And just like that, the conversation ceased, and we got ready.

Sitting there in Emperors' navy and yellow, I listened to Joe welcome me to the team, then give his speech for the game. The pre-game feeling I always got settled over me. The nerves about playing for a new team melted away, and in its place came the determination that had long been my friend over the years. The friend that helped me focus and play the sport I loved.

Tonight, I was going to kick ass and show the fans of Espen exactly what I could do for them.

Chapter 6

Brock

Drinking never held much appeal to me. The only time I'd have a beer was when I was playing football and we won. The guys would go out to celebrate. I'd nurse the same beer all night. It wasn't that I didn't like the taste of it, it was how I felt after. If I was hungover, I didn't practice or play well. That was something I couldn't allow to happen.

Sitting in my living room, watching the Emperors play the Silver Maples, I thought about what others did when they watched games. They drank. Yet, here I sat with a fruit smoothie. Whatever. I'd never been like everyone else. No reason to start now.

Growing up, other kids were scared of me because of my size. They'd move out of my way when they saw me coming. I wasn't that guy, though. I was never a bully. My mom liked to call me a big teddy bear. I always thought that fit my size and personality.

I was sure that was the reason I didn't have many friends. No one wanted to waste their time seeing if there was more beyond my exterior. I was grateful I didn't have to worry about that with Ethan or Lali. They didn't care how big I was. They were my friends no matter what.

The game was going well. The Emperors were up by one. Dominic Truby was on first and Declan was walking to the plate to bat. I didn't know who all the players on the team were but the more popular ones I did. I also followed Callen Teague, Vander Devlin, Ayden Thompson, and Marcus Warner-Wilder more than the others. I loved the dynamic they had with the men they were in love with. The way they didn't shy away from anything out in public. I wanted that. The freedom to be with whomever I chose. And I could have it, now that I was retired, if only I could put myself out there.

My eyes stayed trained on Declan as he lifted the bat and positioned himself so he was ready for the pitch. I looked at his face, his arms, those powerful legs. Now that I knew what he looked like in casual clothes, it was easier to see the man beneath the uniform. The one who lounged on my couch and seemed to love the meals I made for him.

The first pitch was a strike. The second and third were balls. The fourth, he hit with a powerful swing. The ball soared across the field, finding a gap that wasn't covered and sailed into the outfield. By the time the Silver Maples grabbed it—after missing it once—and threw it, Declan was on third and Dominic scored a run.

My smile couldn't have been wider. For Declan's first at bat with the Emperors, he did amazing. I would imagine he'd been nervous. I knew I would be. But Declan was out there like the professional he was and did great.

Unfortunately, he didn't make it to home plate that inning. With two outs already on the board, the next batter struck out, bringing Declan in before he could score.

I watched Declan's games when I could when he was with the Backfins, but there was something different about him playing with the Emperors. Maybe it was the difference in players. I knew he had a friend in Ayden Thompson before he was traded. Maybe it was the difference in the coaching staff or the way the team was run. Whatever it was, it showed in the smile on Declan's face when he made it onto base. He was going to be a hell of an addition to the Emperors.

During the fifth inning, I got up to let Sampson outside to do his business. The land from the front of my house to the dune was fenced. Not that Sampson would wander. He'd always been good at knowing his boundaries, but I liked to keep anyone else walking along the footpath down to the ocean that ran along the side of my property out of my space. I also didn't want to worry about strange people petting my dog. He was friendly but he was big and could be intimidating. My neighbors knew he was a love and petted him when we were out.

Leaning my arms on the railing while keeping my eyes on Sampson, I listened to the waves and watched a handful of people walk up from the beach. Then I heard my name being called.

Glancing over to my right, I saw my neighbor's son. Reed Jessen was the same age as my brother and made it known, since his family moved in two years ago, he was interested in me. I turned him down every time. Gently, because I wasn't a dick. But he was persistent.

"Brock!" He waved and walked to the fence so he could reach over and pet Sampson, who was dutifully waiting for head scratches. Reed glanced up at me and smiled. He reminded me of the typical surfer dude. Light blond hair that was longer, brushing his shoulders. Golden tanned skin. A bright, white smile. Leanly defined muscles. "How are you? I haven't seen you in a few days." Where Reed was standing near the fence line, he didn't have to yell for me to hear him. His voice easily carried up to me.

"I had to help a friend move in. He's staying with me for a while."

I could see the smile slip from Reed's lips. I so did not want to deal with this right now. "A friend?"

"My best friend's brother. He just moved up here. Needed a place to stay for a bit." I didn't want to give away who this friend was. Reed was a fan of all the sports teams Espen had.

When Reed's family first moved in, I offered to help unpack their moving truck. Reed's parents were very friendly and appreciated the assistance. The first time Reed saw me, his steps faltered. I wasn't one of the popular guys on the Sandpipers but I was a solid player. He knew exactly who I was.

"How does Sampson like him?"

I chuckled. "You know he's a whore for attention."

That got Reed to laugh, too.

The TV behind me erupted in a chorus of cheers. I had the slider open with just the screen door closed. The Emperors must have scored. I wanted to rush in there and see who it was but kept my feet planted on the deck. It would be rude to leave Reed mid-conversation.

"Watching the Emperors?" he asked. Of course the sound traveled down to him.

"Yeah, they were up by two last I checked."

"I heard they got a new player. Someone from the Backfins."

I nodded. "Tonight's his first game. Been doing great so far."

"I should go in and watch. I was out with friends and just got home. I saw you standing there so I thought I'd say hi." He looked like he wanted to say more but decided not to voice whatever it was.

I couldn't take him hitting on me much longer. Not once had I given him any inclination that I was gay, but at the same point, the only woman who ever went in and out of my house was Lali. The first time Reed met her, she laughed at the insinuation we were a couple, just like she did when she met Declan. That only fueled Reed on to keep up his persistence to get me to go out with him.

If only I was one of those guys who could say no forcefully and give the impression that it was the end of the discussion. But I wasn't. I was someone who liked to keep the peace. I was nice to everyone around me. Even when someone pissed me off, I had a hard time getting really angry. On the field I was aggressive because I needed to be. It was my job. Off it, I was completely the opposite.

Sampson started his slow walk toward the deck stairs. I took it as my cue to get back inside. I lifted a hand in a wave to Reed. "Have a nice night."

"You, too, Brock."

Once Sampson ambled up the steps, I let him inside and closed the glass slider behind me. He settled on the couch next to me with his head on the arm, looking outside. Even though it was dark, he still liked to keep watch.

The Emperors ended up winning the game by three. Declan didn't score but did get on base again. I couldn't wait to see him hit his first home run for the team.

A couple hours later, as I was getting a drink in the kitchen before heading to bed, I heard footsteps come up from the lower level and the door unlock. Since my house was oceanfront, it was raised up in case it flooded my main living area didn't bear the brunt of it.

When Declan came into the house, the scent of whatever he used as body wash or shampoo reached me first. It had my dick stirring in the basketball shorts I wore, which would do nothing to hide it. I moved so the island was blocking my predicament. Placing my hands on the counter, leaning forward, I willed my body to calm down.

Declan's smile was big when he caught sight of me. "Did you catch the game?"

"I did. You were great tonight."

"Thanks." He went to the fridge and pulled out a bottle of water. I had a front-row seat to watch him tip his head back and down the cool liquid. I got to witness his throat work each swallow.

Down, boy! I internally commanded my dick, which was now halfway hard.

To get my mind off of what it shouldn't be on, I decided to have a little fun with Declan. "Where were you? I figured you would have been home right after the game. It's late."

He slowly lowered the water bottle and leveled me with a glare. "Seriously?"

I shrugged, playing it up like I really cared where he'd been. I didn't. Not in the slightest. He was a grown man, and I wasn't his incredibly overprotective brother. "I just thought you'd be home sooner."

Irritation bled into his tone. "I'm not a child, Brock. If you're going to treat me like one, I'll find somewhere else to stay." He spun on his heel and stalked toward the steps to go upstairs, but I was quick and right behind him. I gripped his elbow, tugging him toward me. He turned, his eyes no longer bright with joy like they were when he got here.

"Dec," I said calmly, making sure my eyes met his. He was only an inch shorter than me. It was nice talking to someone who was nearly as tall as I was. "I didn't mean to upset you. I was only joking."

He slowly pulled his arm from my grasp. "Well, joke about anything you want, just not that. I already have a big brother. I don't need another one."

"I'm sorry. Honest. I would never want to upset you."

Seconds ticked by while he searched my face, no doubt making sure I was sincere. "Yeah, okay. I don't like being smothered and watched over constantly. I was hoping you wouldn't spy on me and relay my moves to Ethan."

"I would never break your trust like that. The way I see it, you're not a kid anymore." Didn't I know it. "You're grown and a professional baseball player. You didn't have anyone watching over you in Maryland, you won't here. That doesn't mean I care any less, but I won't be in your business all the time. If I was truly worried about you, I have your number. I could have texted you. I might be close with Ethan, but you living here isn't so I can watch you. It's to offer you a place to stay while you're in between homes."

He swallowed and I was helpless to look away. What was it about this man's neck that had me so intrigued? He nodded, drawing my gaze back to his face. "Glad we got that out in the open."

"Me, too."

"Are you going to bed now?"

"I was going to. Why? Did you need something?"

He turned toward the living room. "Nah, it's okay."

"Dec, I have nowhere to be tomorrow. What's up?"

"Want to play a little Madden on the Xbox?"

I chuckled. "Still jacked up from your first game?"

"Yeah, I can't sleep yet."

"Let's go."

Just like that, the tension was gone as Declan and I sat on the couch, with Sampson on the floor, while we played a game where neither of us could get hurt. That was my kind of football these days.

Chapter 7

Declan

The salty sea breeze blew across my face. There was still a slight chill in the air in the early morning, which was only made worse by being out in the middle of the Delaware Bay on the ferry. Finally, after a week of Uber and rides, we were on our way down to get my car. I'd missed the freedom of being able to go wherever I wanted, whenever I wanted, without waiting for a ride.

Of course, Brock had offered me the use of his SUV. It just didn't feel right constantly leaving him without a way to get around if he needed to go somewhere, while his vehicle sat in the parking lot of the Emperors stadium for hours at a time.

Brock leaned over the railing, the coffee we'd stopped for on the way down still in his hand. The sun made the dark strands of his hair look lighter than they did in the lights of his home. Why was I noticing shit like that? I knew why, but I didn't want to notice it. Fuck. I wasn't fourteen anymore, watching Brock while hanging out with him and my brother. Twenty-six was entirely too old to still have a teenage crush.

I could tell myself that shit all I wanted. Apparently, while I thought I'd matured and moved on, my brain and dick had other ideas, as the extra time in the shower to get myself off could attest to. His scent surrounded me everywhere I went in the house. The power it held over me grew when we climbed into the car together this morning. A quick ride to the stadium was nothing compared to an hour being encased in the same small space. By the time we reached the line to board the ferry, I was shocked he hadn't noticed my dick straining against the zipper of my shorts.

The moment he put the SUV in park, I'd leapt out of it, feigning the need for a bathroom. Really, I just needed some fresh air to clear my head. With still another hour on the other side of the ferry, I convinced him to stay on the deck for the entire ride. No way would I sink low enough to jerk off in a public bathroom, which left me with the fresh salt air to clear my senses.

"What are you thinking about over there?"

"Nothing. Just enjoying the peaceful sea breeze surrounding us."

He straightened and turned to face me. "I wouldn't describe your glare at the water below as peaceful."

"I wasn't glaring."

He smirked. "You were and that usually means you're upset about something."

I leaned on the railing, facing Brock. "So living with me for a week means you've figured out all of my tells."

After the misunderstanding the night I played my first game with the Emperors, Brock and I'd found an even footing. I didn't jump to conclusions about his motivations for his concern and he didn't hover over me like my brother would have. It had been my fault for taking his teasing remarks as him watching over me. He also understood why I felt that way. Now that we'd cleared the air, we'd gotten into a comfortable routine.

When we were both home, we ate our meals together. Brock hadn't been kidding when he said he liked to cook. There were so many different things he could make. Thankfully, he focused on healthy eating. With how good everything was, I'd need extra hours in the gym to work it all off.

"No, I didn't need to figure them out. They haven't changed since you were younger." He walked over to the trash can and tossed the coffee cup in. "Whenever you had something on your mind growing up, you'd stare off into space, glaring at nothing in particular."

No way would I, or could I, admit what the problem was. How was I supposed to tell Brock that my crush on him as a kid had reared its head again after only a week of living with him? It wasn't even like he was into men. I really doubted the straight guy wanted to know the bi guy had a thing for him. Especially, when he'd been kind enough to let me stay in his house instead of dealing with a hotel. I didn't need to make things awkward for him, which meant I needed to get my little infatuation under control.

"Just thinking how long it's been since I've driven my baby." Fuck, that sounded shallow.

"That attached to your car?"

"Not just any car. It's the first high-end car I bought with my own money." The reason why the car meant so much to me was true. I'd been a Major League Baseball player for four years. In all that time I'd been very cautious with my money. Ethan convinced me to save most of my salary in case I got hurt and couldn't play anymore. My only two extravagant purchases for myself had been my home and my car. Ethan hadn't wanted me to help him buy a home and all my parents wanted were upgrades on theirs.

"I get it. I feel the same way about my house."

A low beep filled the air. "Attention all passengers, please start making your way back to your vehicles. We will be docking shortly."

Passengers from all over the ship started to emerge from the interior areas on their way to the stairwells that would return them to the lower parts of the ship and their cars. Curious eyes darted our way as people passed, probably trying to figure out who Brock was. It wasn't always easy to recognize football players without their helmets and jerseys, especially the linemen.

"Aren't you Declan Armitage?" one guy asked over his shoulder just before walking by.

"I am." I looked at Brock then back at the guy.

"Oh my god. You had a great game the other night. I'm thrilled with the Emperors trade to get you. Would you mind signing something for me?"

"I'd be happy to." In Maryland, this kind of thing happened to me all the time. I'd expected it to take longer for the fans in Espen to warm up to their former enemy.

I scribbled my name across the guy's T-shirt where he indicated and waved as he walked away. Brock and I took the stairs down to the lower level.

It wasn't until we were inside his SUV that I asked the question on my mind. "Why would that guy want my autograph and not yours? You played in Espen a helluva lot longer than me."

Brock started the SUV while the deckhands used the ropes to anchor the ferry to the dock. "Most people don't recognize me. I played hard, but all the recognition in football goes to the people who score the points, which is more than fine with me."

"You don't like the limelight?"

The cars in front of us started off the ferry. Brock inched along behind them. "No. I played to help my family. The last thing I wanted was the press in my business. I kept my head down and my mind on training, practice, or the next game." He drove off the ferry, looking in both directions before crossing the road and merging onto the highway. "You don't seem to mind it, though."

I glanced out the window, watching the familiar sights in front of me. "Baseball is different. There's only nine of us on the field. Each and every one of us are in the limelight. I guess I've learned to live with people being in my business. It's part of the job."

"Is the job worth it, though?"

That pulled up the corners of my mouth. "Every minute of it. I love everything about the game. I honestly don't know what I'd do without baseball."

"I never felt that way about football. It was a career like anything else. It wasn't some lifelong dream."

I looked over at Brock. "Did you like playing football at all?"

"I did, but didn't love it. Plus, I was good at what I did. It just wasn't what I wanted to do with the rest of my life."

I'd known Brock had finished his degree in psychology, even after he'd been drafted into the NFL. If I had to guess, he wanted to do something in that field for his career. I couldn't imagine a life where I had to do something other than what I loved. What kind of way was that to live? Though I could see why and how Brock would be good at football. His sheer size gave him an advantage as a front-line player. Smaller than when he was playing, Brock was still a big, muscular man.

My gaze drew down his body and all thoughts about what he'd wanted to do with his life were derailed. The strong muscles of his shoulders stretching the fabric of his T-shirt. The scruff on his chin and cheeks. Brock's earthy scent filling the SUV. This would be a long fucking hour to my garage. At least once we were there, I'd be able to ride back alone and clear my thoughts before we returned to his house.

Brock was the kind of man who hit all of my buttons. Strong enough to hold me down and fuck me into the mattress, but also man enough to let me do the same to him. It was more than that. Brock was still the same guy who helped me with my homework and made me feel included, even when there were years separating him from me. Brock was a gentle giant who deserved happiness in his life. Hopefully, someday he'd find the right woman to give him that.

I adjusted my position in the seat, trying to hide my rock-hard cock from his sight. One hour, that was all I needed to keep it together for.

"What time do you have to be at the stadium today?"

"Around three. I brought my bag with me, just in case I need to go right there when we get back."

Brock nodded. "Should we grab lunch before we head home? I'd be willing to bet the food on the ship is pretty bad."

"I know the perfect place when we get into town."

"Feeling a little nostalgic?"

I smiled and looked out the front window. "You could say that. It's not like I'll never be here again. We play the Backfins multiple times during the season."

"I'm glad you came to Espen, Dec."

We lapsed into silence again, only the sounds from the radio filling the space. I did my best to bring up random conversations here and there. When we were home alone, the conversation flowed so naturally. Here, trapped in his SUV, it felt stilted. And all of the tension came from me. If we weren't talking, I was focused on Brock. Every breath he took. Each movement of his arms when he switched lanes or exited the highway.

By the time we arrived at my old place, my stomach was in a ball of knots. I stepped out of the SUV and discreetly adjusted myself. I walked around the back of the house where the detached garage sat. It was still off-limits for the realtor. After today I'd be able to give the office the code, now that my car was with me. I punched in the numbers and waited as the door lifted.

The silver of the hood gleamed in the light as the garage door reached the top. Brock whistled behind me.

"That is a beautiful car."

I ran my hand along the side of it. "She is, isn't she?"

Brock chuckled. "Do you treat your women the same way you treat your car?"

I turned to Brock and hit the unlock button over my shoulder. "I treat my women *and* my men that way."

A strange look passed over Brock's face before he schooled his features. He knew I was bi. Hopefully, the reminder that I slept with both men and women didn't freak him out.

"Brock, are you okay?"

"Hmmm? Yeah, just hungry." He looked at the time on his phone. "We better get on the road so you can get to the stadium in time." Brock moved back over to the driver's door of his SUV. "I'll follow you to the restaurant."

A heaviness settled into my chest. I wanted to grill him on his strange reaction to my comment about men and women. Earlier today, I was more than ready to have a few hours alone in my car to get the scent of Brock off my mind. Now, as I climbed inside, watching Brock do the same, I wished I was back in there with him.

Chapter 8

Brock

I wished I was one of those people who could sleep in late. I wasn't. The longest I could stay in bed was nine hours and that was rare. Most days, I was up between seven and eight without setting an alarm. My body had its own internal one.

The sun was shining and there wasn't a cloud in the sky. I sipped my coffee as I leaned my elbows on the deck railing while Sampson was out sniffing the sand, trying to find the perfect spot to go to the bathroom. People were already walking down the path alongside my house so they could get a good spot on the beach.

Memorial Day weekend was when the crowds started picking up here. I had a love/hate relationship with it. On the one hand, it meant warmer, longer days. I wasn't a fan of the cold of winter, so this was my favorite time of year. On the other, I didn't like the crowds or the traffic or the noise. I could have bought a lot of acres and lived inland without another home in sight. The extra visitors were worth the view I got here every day.

It was a good thing Declan had the day off. Trying to get to the stadium today would have been a nightmare.

"Hey, Brock!" I heard coming from my right. Turning, I found Reed on his deck, coffee in hand. Why was he awake at this time of the morning? He should have been out partying with his friends last night and sleeping in.

I waved. "Surprised you're up this early!"

He just shrugged and smiled before he dropped into the zero-gravity chair on his deck and stretched out. Reed was bare chested, showing off the visible six-pack of muscles he had. He scratched his stomach as he sipped his coffee. That hand dipped a little lower to the top of his board shorts.

The sliding door behind me opened, snapping my gaze away from Reed. I should not have been looking at him like that. Ever. But it was like he was putting on a show. No, I didn't want to date him, but a man could only take so much temptation before he had to look. And I was sure Reed knew what he was doing.

Turning, I saw Declan come outside with a cup of coffee as well. His hair was standing up all over the place. "You just can't sleep in, can you?" he asked with his sleep roughened voice. It wasn't sexy. Not in the slightest. Neither were his cotton sleep shorts or his T-shirt that looked so soft I wanted to rub my cheek against it.

I focused on Sampson again. He had made his way over to the fence where Reed was cooing to him from his deck.

Before I could answer Declan, he asked, "Jesus, who's that?"

My body tensed as I stood up straight. "No one you need to worry about."

Declan turned to me, a curious, yet somewhat unhappy look on his face. "I'll be the one who decides that."

When I looked toward Reed again, he'd climbed down the stairs to the sand and was petting Sampson's head. Was he a ninja? How did he move so fast?

Reed's eyes were on Declan. No, this wasn't going to happen. No way was I going to allow the two of them to hook up. Hold on, why was I getting jealous? Declan wasn't mine. I didn't want anything sexual with Reed. They were closer to each other in age. It wouldn't be a bad match. But I couldn't sit by and watch it happen for some reason.

I nudged Declan. "Come on. I'll make you breakfast."

"Are you Brock's new roommate?" Reed called up. *Here we go.*

"I am," Declan responded.

"Be good to Brock. He's one of the best men I know."

My tension deflated and my shoulders sagged. Reed was a good guy. I was being awful.

Declan's eyes were on me again, but this time I ducked my head, not wanting to see what was swimming in them. "That he is." I felt his hand gently lay on my arm, drawing my gaze to his. "Breakfast?"

I swallowed hard. "Right. Come on, Sampson. Stop being a whore." Two people on the footpath stopped to stare at me. I must have said that louder than I intended. "Sorry! Was talking to my dog!"

Declan chuckled. I hated tourist season.

Back inside the house, I pulled out pans to make omelets. As they were warming up, I chopped up a bunch of vegetables. I ate two of these on my own. I made Declan's in one pan while I started mine in another. I had a lot of his food preferences memorized after the short period of time he'd been here.

He took a seat at the island. "So, you're neighbor..." He left the sentence hanging, leaving me unsure about what his next words would have been.

"He's the same age as Wyatt."

"Okay. Do you have something against him?"

"No, he's an okay guy. Just young." I couldn't lie and say Reed was a terrible human being. He wasn't. He was nice, friendly, warm, inviting, and attractive. But that didn't mean I wanted Declan running over there to hang out with him. "I'm surprised he didn't recognize you. He keeps up with all the Espen teams."

"I'm not exactly looking my best at the moment."

I turned to face him. "You look fine to me." Better than fine. He was gorgeous all sleep rumpled, sitting in my kitchen like he was meant to be here. I needed to bite my tongue and make breakfast.

We didn't speak again until I had the plates set down on the table with glasses of juice and coffee.

"I'm going to go down to the beach when we're done," Declan spoke after devouring half his breakfast. "Get some beach time in before it gets busier."

"That's smart. It's going to get crazy."

"You want to come?"

"No, I like to go at night when there's next to no one there. I can take Sampson down and let him chase the little crabs that pop up from the sand."

He chuckled. "I'll have to go back with you later to see that."

We kept the conversation light. No more talk of Reed, for which I was grateful. After we cleaned up from breakfast, Declan went upstairs to change while I debated on what to do. I wasn't getting in my Toyota and leaving. That was a hard pass. No way did I want to sit in traffic. I didn't want to be on the deck with all the people coming and going either.

Declan stopped next to the couch where I was sitting with Sampson on one side of me. He seriously needed to put on a shirt. It took everything in me to will my eyes up to Declan's face. He had muscles that went on for miles. So perfectly defined, I wanted to lick them.

"You sure you don't want to go?" He had combed his hair, so it was back to looking perfect as usual. The slight scruff on his jaw was entirely too enticing.

"I'm good." My voice came out huskier than I intended. I cleared my throat. "Thanks for asking."

"If you change your mind, I'll be close by."

"You know you'll be recognized." It wasn't easy for me to blend in, given my size, but I wasn't an Emperor. Declan was sure to see fans on the beach, especially with more than the locals there.

He shrugged. "It's fine. If it gets to be too much, I'll come back."

I nodded. "Have fun."

I kept my gaze on the windows instead of on Declan's backside as he made his way to the door. I did not follow him with my eyes as he walked along the path. I did not stand and tempt myself until he disappeared out of view.

Those were lies. I did all of those things. I needed an intervention. Or to get laid. By someone other than Declan.

I growled and raked a hand through my hair. "This is all your fault," I told Sampson. He lifted his head. "It's not but I need someone to blame." I dropped down on the couch and kept talking to the dog like he had advice he was going to give me. "What am I going to do? I can't lust after Dec."

What I needed was something to keep me busy. I stood and went up to my bedroom to grab my laptop then resumed my spot next to the dog. Once it powered on, I started browsing colleges, even Espen University. I'd been thinking about maybe going back to further my education.

An hour went by as I scrolled from page to page then site to site. I was getting nowhere. My mind wasn't on this. It was on the man down on the beach.

"Screw it."

Closing the lid to the laptop, I put it on the small, round table near the end of the couch and stood. I shouldn't have fought it. It was inevitable I would end up on the beach with Declan. No matter how much I tried to keep my distance from him, when he was in my orbit—in my home—I was the proverbial moth, and he was the flame. There was nowhere else I wanted to be but near him.

Foul Ball

After changing into a pair of navy board shorts, I slipped a different shirt on and grabbed a big beach towel. I had no plans to go into the water. If I did, I would have put on a swim shirt that wouldn't cling to me like a second skin if it got wet.

"Be good," I told Sampson before grabbing my single house key with the clip on it that I easily hooked on my belt loop. I kept this one strictly for use when I went down to the beach. I didn't bother with my phone, leaving it on the counter.

With the door locked and my flip-flops on, I made my way along the path to the beach. There were people everywhere, but it wasn't to the point where they were on top of each other.

It didn't take long to find Declan. He was running back on a clear path of beach with a football in his hand, getting ready to toss it to someone.

Wait. Was that Reed?

Without thinking, I started trekking through the warm sand until I got to Reed, since he was closer. My towel was fisted tightly in my hand. I seriously needed to get a grip on this whole Reed and Declan thing. It was not only none of my business, but I couldn't have Declan myself. He was free to date whoever he wanted. Except I didn't want him to date Reed.

"Brock!" Reed shouted when he noticed me. He threw his arms around my neck to hug me when I got close. I forgot how he liked to show affection. It was another reason I kept my distance from him. I patted his shoulder blade but didn't embrace him back.

Reed introduced me to his friends, who I vaguely remembered meeting before, but my gaze kept straying to Declan as he jogged closer. When he stopped next to us, I was drawn to the sweat glistening on his chest. Quickly, I turned back to Reed to keep from getting hard in front of everyone.

How was I supposed to stay away from Declan when he looked like he belonged on the cover of *Sports Illustrated*? He had to be the hottest player in the majors.

Reed placed his hand on my bicep, giving it a little squeeze. "I didn't know Declan Armitage was your roommate. You two grew up together?"

I nodded, not sure how much Declan had told him. "Dec's brother is my best friend. Our families have been close for a long time."

The way Reed kept his eyes on me let me know he wasn't interested in Declan. I glanced back to Declan and found him watching Reed.

I gently shook Reed off and walked away, finding Declan's towel nearby to put mine down next to, then sat on it. I was done socializing, even if it was rude to walk away from Reed. I needed some space.

Yet that space didn't come. Because two point four seconds later, Declan sat beside me and started drinking from his water bottle, drawing me right to his neck. I was sure if I licked it, I'd taste the salt on his skin. My mouth watered at the sight. I should have brought my own bottle of water down with me. It would have given me something to do.

"Reed's fun," Declan said once he was done drinking.

It took a moment for my brain to get back on track and away from anything that made me hard. "Yeah, he's a nice kid."

"He's not a kid, Brock. He's only four years younger than me."

"It's easier if I think of him as one."

"You got a thing for him?" His tone wasn't joking but held a serious edge to it.

"What? No. He keeps trying to get me to go out with him, though. I'm not interested. He's not my type." My type was apparently sitting right next me, smelling like sweat, salt, and rock-hard man. Why did I think coming down here was a good idea?

"There are a lot of women out here. I'm sure any one of them would be happy to go home with you."

I grunted in response. Declan deserved to know the truth about me but here was neither the time nor the place. Plus, I had to build up the courage to tell him. That was the most difficult part. Saying those words I'd only ever spoken to two other people.

When I went to bars under disguise to hook up, I didn't need words. Just actions. Here, with Declan, actions wouldn't do. Well, in my fantasies they would, not in real life. I also didn't know how he'd react once he knew. Would he feel like I was deliberately keeping it from him? That I didn't trust him?

Declan nudged me with his shoulder. I thought he was about to say something else but then a guy came over to get his autograph. At least that put an end to the conversation.

Chapter 9

Declan

"Fuck, we pulled that win out of our asses." Callen yanked open the door to the locker room.

He wasn't joking. Down by four runs in the ninth, we had one last at bat to pull the game out of the gutter. With our bats all but absent for the first eight innings, I didn't have a lot of faith we could get the win. I forgot I wasn't in Maryland anymore.

One out and the round-robin of hits started. Only one home run through the entire inning. It seemed all the hits we should have had throughout the game piled into the end. Dominic ended the rally with a double, bringing in the last two runs and putting us up by one for the win. The Backfins never would have been able to get out of their heads to bat, down by that many. The Emperors were an entirely different story. The challenge seemed to excite them.

"I'm sure you're all pulling many things out of your asses, but that shit was skill." Dominic flexed his muscles, kissing his bicep in a move worthy of a weight lifter or a porn star.

If I'd learned anything in the almost two weeks I'd been here, it was that Dominic did not have a filter and said whatever popped into his brain at the moment, no matter how ridiculous or inappropriate it might be. Vander wasn't much better, but he usually saved his shit to give right back to Dominic.

Vander opened his mouth and Callen shook his head. "Don't do it. He hit in the winning run. He's going to be in rare form the rest of the night. It won't be worth the mental effort when he devolves into fart and poop jokes like a middle schooler." Callen tossed his jersey into the laundry bin on the way to his locker.

No way was I getting in the middle of that. I wanted to get out of here and relax after such a stressful game.

"Ignore them. They'll bicker for a bit and then get their shit together." Ayden walked up next to me. "While they continue with their nonsense, how about we get showered and head out for a late lunch?"

I tugged off my jersey, the white practically yellow from my slide into third earlier in the game, and threw it toward the laundry bin. I always felt bad for the crew who'd have to get the stains out for the next game.

"I'm down for lunch, but don't you want to get home to Rome since we have an early night?"

"We do, but Rome doesn't. The Jetties are launching some new team promo and Katie needs Rome to work late. So a late lunch with you sounds better than going home alone."

I lifted a brow. "I'm your back-up date?"

Ayden gave me a soft punch to the shoulder. "No, ass. We just haven't had a chance to really catch up since you got here."

I smirked. "Lunch sounds good."

Marcus burst out laughing. "Vander, you should give up while you're ahead."

I didn't hear what Dominic and Vander were joking back and forth about and I didn't want to know. I pulled off my cleats and the rest of my clothes and went right to the shower. Ayden would want to be home before Rome got there. I noticed him hot on my heels.

"Smart move," he said before ducking into one of the shower stalls.

By the time I stepped out of the shower and came back into the main locker room area, the crowd had thinned. Ayden and a few others, who escaped to the showers at the same time we had, were getting dressed. Everyone else had probably just started getting cleaned up.

Ayden tugged his bag up on his shoulder as he approached. "Ready?"

"Yeah." I picked up my own. "Where did you want to go?"

"Let's show you some new places in town."

I followed Ayden out to the parking lot, where he climbed behind the wheel of a Jaguar SUV. "Follow me, I know the perfect place."

"Will do." I slide in behind the wheel of my Mercedes, reveling in the smell of the leather. I'd missed not driving my baby while it waited for me in Maryland.

Ayden kept the pace slow so I wouldn't get lost on the unfamiliar streets. Sure, I knew how to get from Brock's to the stadium and back again without the GPS, but everything else had been a bit more difficult. Probably since I hadn't traveled much outside of the stadium and Brock's. No need to. He had everything you could ask for at his home.

Ayden pulled into the lot of the Espen Steakhouse. It sounded like a place I'd need to visit more often. I drove up to the front and put the car in park before climbing out and handing my keys to the valet. Once I had my ticket, I followed Ayden. The hostess walked up to us as soon as we stepped inside.

"Welcome back, Mr. Thompson. No Mr. Thompson today?"

Ayden smiled and shook his head. "No, Rome's working late tonight." He gestured to me. "This is my friend, Declan—"

"Declan Armitage. Right fielder." A warm smiled filled her face. "Welcome to Espen. Great game you guys had today."

"Thank you. It's great being here."

"Let me show you to your table." She picked up two menus and started through the restaurant.

She stopped at a table off to the side that offered a bit of privacy. I always loved restaurants that took our desire to have a meal in private seriously. There were many times when the host or hostess would seat us in the middle of the room, giving the rest of their customers the chance to gawk at us, eavesdrop on our conversations, and interrupt our meals for autographs.

It was nice to find somewhere that wanted to give us a chance to eat without the fanfare.

"Thanks, Annette. This is perfect."

"You're welcome. Your waiter will be over in a moment."

Ayden took his menu from Annette. "Great."

As she handed me mine, her smile grew a little brighter before she let go and walked away.

Ayden's head was buried deep in his menu, but that didn't stop his voice from carrying to me. "Man, would she love to go out with you."

"Maybe." I opened my own menu. "Not that I'm looking to date anyone right now. I'm still trying to get my feet under me here." *And a certain straight man out of my thoughts.*

"You wouldn't take someone out who showed the slightest bit of interest? I have to say, I'm shocked."

I looked up from the menu to find Ayden watching me. "Don't get me wrong. I've had plenty of offers, just not interested yet."

"Men or women?"

I laughed. "Oh, so now that you've decided to join me on the bisexual side, you want to dig into my sex life?"

"I've always been nosey as fuck when it comes to your sex life. You just never give many details."

I shrugged. "Who am I to sleep with and tell?"

That made Ayden laugh. The waiter came over seconds later to take our orders. With our meals and drinks picked out, the waiter walked away to put in the ticket. He retuned almost instantly with our drinks.

"What do you think of Espen so far?" Ayden asked,

"Different. I've seen the traffic we get in the summer, but it was nothing compared to what you had to deal with the other day. I was thrilled we had off and I wasn't going to have to drive through that mess."

"Yeah. It's pretty bad this time of year. The Fourth of July will be even worse."

I groaned and lifted the glass to my lips. "Don't tell me that."

"Shouldn't be too bad with Brock living oceanfront."

"It's not. I was able to walk down to the beach yesterday with no problems."

"The one downfall with living outside of town, having to drive into the mess to get to the beach."

I rolled my eyes. "Yep. It's such a hardship having to sit by your pool all day."

"It is, especially when I try to get Rome out of that little Speedo of his."

I lifted my hand up. "Nope. You're not going to give me details about you fucking your husband in your pool."

He winked. "You're right. I'd only do that to Dominic to fuck with him. Now, tell me, how's the roommate situation going?"

"Good, actually. Brock loves to cook and doesn't feel the need to watch over every move I make like Ethan does."

"That's a plus," Ayden said. "I was worried your brother would want Brock to keep tabs on you while you were staying there."

The waiter delivered our meals and quickly disappeared. I really loved this place.

"I'm sure Ethan asked, but knowing Brock, he told him no. It's not his style."

"Well, if you ever need a different place to stay, the offer still stands."

I smiled at my friend. The connection we made in college couldn't be broken, no matter which team we played on. "I know. Thanks."

Talking almost stopped as we each dug into the steaks on our plate. Famished from the game, neither of us seemed to want to stop eating to dive deep into further conversation. We talked more about Espen and playing for the Emperors while we lingered over our drinks.

It was nice to catch up with Ayden one-on-one, especially when I knew he wouldn't be leaving for a new city the next day. I'd missed my friend. Now, we wouldn't have to wait so long between our times together. I also knew that having Ayden around would give me someone to talk to. And if I couldn't get my brain off of lusting after Brock soon, I was definitely going to need to call in help.

Brock and Sampson were nowhere to be seen when I walked through the front door. It was late enough that I knew he could have Sampson down at the beach. He liked avoiding the crowds, and without the lifeguards, he didn't have to worry about anyone asking him to take Sampson off the beach. I'd showered at the stadium, but a pair of gym shorts and a T-shirt sounded heavenly at the moment.

I climbed the stairs and dumped my bag on my bed. It wasn't long before I shed the jeans and shirt I wore for something immensely more comfortable. Feeling more relaxed, I figured I'd take a walk down toward the water to find Sampson and Brock.

About halfway down the stairs, I heard Brock's voice trail up to me. No need to find them, they'd apparently gotten back. My foot froze on the step when I heard my name being spoken. What the fuck? Brock had promised not to tell my brother everything about me living here. I figured the only way I could confront Brock about this bullshit was if I heard the conversation he was having over the phone.

I stayed exactly where I was and waited.

"What if he's angry and leaves when he finds out? I don't want him to go," he said.

Well, that was going to be tough shit. If he couldn't keep his promise about leaving my brother out of the loop, I was out of here.

Brock's voice was low. "You know how hard it is for me."

Apparently, he didn't mean ratting me out to my brother. He'd done that without blinking.

"I know being gay isn't a big deal, but it's not something that's easy for me to say out loud," he continued.

Brock is gay?

Did my brother know? Had they kept the secret from me? I'd spent all of my teenage years lusting after a guy I thought was straight. A man, whose body and voice still turned me on. And here I was feeling guilty for wanting a straight man when it seemed that man was anything but straight.

"I know. Thank you. I'm glad I have you in my corner."

The room grew quiet, but my heart was racing in my chest. How did I not know? These were questions I certainly wanted answers to.

"Bye."

When it was clear Brock had ended the call, I forced my feet to move down the rest of the stairs. I stepped behind the couch where Brock lay sideways across it. I crossed my arms over my chest and addressed the man who had been keeping too many secrets. "You're gay?"

Chapter 10

Brock

Fuck! Shit! Cocksucking motherfucker!

I wasn't someone who swore much, except when I was feeling some sort of strong emotion, like I was in this very moment.

Maybe if I would have checked to see if Declan was home before I talked to Lali this wouldn't have happened. Or if I would have talked to her behind the closed door of my bedroom. But I wasn't apparently smart enough to do any of that.

So here I was, lying on the couch with an irritated Declan hovering next to me. Sampson decided he didn't need to be here for this and left. Figured.

Thanks for the support, buddy!

Sitting up, I scrubbed my hand over my face. If I was going to have this conversation, which apparently I was, I didn't want to do it on my back because all that did was make me imagine Declan lying on top of me after he found out I was gay. This was not the time for fantasies.

When I finally was brave enough to meet his eyes, I asked, "How was the game?" I knew. I watched it.

"I don't think so." Declan wasn't going to let me get out of this.

"Well, at least have a seat so I don't have to keep craning my neck to look at you."

He dropped down, leaving a few feet between us. He didn't sit on the other side of the huge sectional. I called it a win. "Talk."

This was it. I was going to tell Declan about me, except for the fact that I wanted him badly. That wouldn't enter into this conversation. But I was going to speak the words I said to only two other people. The ones he heard, even though I didn't mean for him to. At least I didn't have to figure out a way to do this. It was out there. What I needed to do now was come clean.

"I'm gay."

"No shit. I heard that much. How long have you known?"

"I don't remember the exact age. Just that one day when my friends were looking at girls and talking about how pretty they were, I was looking at boys. Then I was comparing the two. Trying to figure out why I was different than them. Why I couldn't see what the big deal was with the opposite sex."

"And my brother?"

I reeled back. "In no way, shape, or form am I attracted to Ethan."

He rolled his eyes. "That's not what I meant. You were just talking to him, so obviously he knows."

"I was on the phone with Lali not Ethan. But yes, he knows."

"Who else?"

"Just the two of them."

"You're telling me, over all these years, you never told another soul you're gay?"

I shook my head.

"How is that even possible? Are you a virgin?"

And here we were wading into territory I didn't want to be in with Declan. Sure, I wanted to touch him, kiss him, feel his muscles contract as I dragged my tongue over them, but I didn't need to vocalize how many sexual partners I'd had, but since we were getting everything out there...

"I'm not a virgin. I've been with enough men to know it's what I prefer."

"How have you been hooking up without the media catching on?"

"I wear disguises. But I haven't been with anyone since retiring."

Declan watched me for a moment, as if he was looking for any sign I was lying. I wasn't. I might not have been completely truthful, but it wasn't a lie, simply an omission. The last guy I'd been with was probably two years ago.

I didn't like hookups; however, they were a necessity. I hated not being able to be myself. Then there was the emptiness that followed each encounter. We both got each other off and went our separate ways. There was no intimacy, no connection. That was what I longed for. Not getting my dick sucked or having a quickie and turning away just to find another willing body when I wanted it again.

"All this time in the NFL, the years that have gone by, how could you keep it quiet?"

"I was afraid if everyone knew, I would be treated differently, not just by management, but those I played with in college and the Sandpipers. I'd heard some of the guys in the locker rooms. Homophobia didn't run rampant, but it existed. What if I would have come out and my game suffered? What if my teammates didn't treat me the same on the field? Or I lost fans or the backing of my coaches? Endorsements? I needed to keep playing so I could keep making money. You know what it was like for me growing up. We didn't have much. When I was in the NFL, I was able to give my family whatever they wanted. I couldn't jeopardize that."

Dropping my head, I looked down at my hand where it was still holding my phone. I wasn't ashamed of where I came from or how hard I worked to get to where I was. I was proof it was possible to do well, no matter what my financial situation was. My parents never let money define who we were as a family. They were loving and kind to everyone around them. I was proud to be a Richmond. In return, I wanted them to be proud to have me as their son.

"Do your parents and Wyatt know?"

"No."

Declan placed his hand on my thigh. The warmth of it seeped through the thin material of my shorts. "Brock," he said gently. Hearing my name from his lips nearly did me in.

I lifted my gaze to his, not sure what I'd see there. I hadn't known Declan well in years. Yes, I remembered the boy in high school then the man he grew into in college and beyond, but I wasn't close with him then. I didn't know him inside and out like I did Ethan. Even living here for a couple weeks, I still hadn't fully figured him out.

"You're done playing professionally. You don't have to hide anymore. While I don't think you should have while you were playing, I understand where you're coming from. I didn't let many know I was bi until Callen came out. But that's in the past. You could find someone to be with now."

"Easier said than done. Lali's been trying to get me out of the house. She said she'd be my wingwoman and go to a gay bar with me. But I don't want to fool around with a stranger. I want to get to know the person first. What if they're only after me for who I am? Not that I was a big player on the Sandpipers, but I wasn't a nobody. How do I know who I can trust?" What I didn't say was what was in my heart. This wasn't just about getting off. I wanted the possibility of love.

"Find someone you know who won't be a dick."

"I'm not sleeping with your brother."

"One, ewww. I don't want to think about my brother sleeping with anyone. Two, since my brother is into T and A, I didn't mean him."

"Well, considering only three people know at the moment and one of them is definitely female..."

"God, you're so dense right now."

I wasn't, though. I just didn't want to think about what he was implying. Didn't want to imagine that kind of reality because it was everything I wanted, yet knew I couldn't have.

"Me, Brock." He grinned, his hand never leaving my thigh. "We could have some fun together." Then his thumb started brushing along the fabric of my shorts, sending a bolt of electricity right up to my balls.

I jumped up, knowing if I didn't, I was going to be hard in seconds. Declan was basically laying himself out there like the buffet I never wanted to stop sampling from. And that wasn't going to happen. I had the promise I made to Ethan rattling around my head, reminding me I couldn't touch Declan, no matter how badly I wanted to.

"No," I said, though it came out way huskier than I intended. I wanted it to be firm and final, putting an end to this conversation. So much for that.

Not at all fazed by my rejection, Declan stood and came within a breath away from me. I could feel his body heat radiating off him. Smell the scent of the body wash he used after every game. And those eyes... Hazel but sometimes they'd go a little more green. Today they were bright and leaning green. I was losing myself in them until I felt his hand on my forearm.

"It would work for both of us," he prodded, pulling me from my thoughts.

"I can't." Before he could ask me why, I spoke again. "It wouldn't be smart. You're staying here and soon you'll be leaving for your own place. Besides, I'm not looking for someone to fool around with." I hoped he didn't say this could be more than that. It would throw my excuse right out the window. I did want a relationship, although it wasn't the main reason I was turning him down. He didn't need to know that. I could never tell him I promised his brother I wouldn't touch him.

"Consider it your warm-up to getting out there in the dating game. You could use me for practice." Oh, how I wanted to use him, but I could never do that. I had a feeling deep in my gut that if I touched Declan once, I'd never be able to stop.

"Declan..." I warned low.

He leaned close like he was about to kiss me, but I turned my head so those perfect lips of his grazed my cheek. When he pulled back, he smirked. "I'm not going to push you anymore right now. Think about it. I'm here. You're gay. I'm bi. We could spend my time here getting off. No reason for us to not take advantage of our proximity and attraction to one another." Before I could tell him no again, he turned and grabbed his phone before slipping outside.

I moved to the sliding door, watching as he went to the beach. He stopped before he was on the other side of the small dune and turned, as if sensing my gaze on him. I didn't step away, no matter how much I wanted to. I also wondered if he saw me since the windows had a light reflective tint to them to help with privacy and to keep some of the sun out of the house. Maybe he could feel my eyes on him. Either way, I didn't move until he was gone from sight.

I collapsed onto the couch, mirroring the pose Declan found me in when I unknowingly confessed my sexuality to him. I could still feel his touch, no matter how gentle. A ghost of a sensation I didn't want to forget. It was all I'd allow myself to have. No way could I have anything with Declan. Ethan would hand me my ass. I couldn't go behind his back and break my promise, even though it was tempting to do so.

And Declan... He wasn't some random guy I'd picked up in a club. He was family, even if we weren't related. He was someone who'd been in my life for as long as I could remember. Someone who no amount of time or miles apart could break that familiarity of having him nearby again.

No, I couldn't do this.

My thoughts wandered to my parents and my brother. I needed to tell them, but I wasn't ready. Having Declan find out today was enough. There was only so much I could take at one time.

If I really thought about it, which I had more times than I could count, I didn't think my family would care that I was gay. They would support me like they had done my entire life. That didn't mean it was any easier to say the words. To reveal this part of myself I got so used to hiding. I'd tell them soon.

Sampson got up from his spot on the floor and came over to nudge me with his snout. I petted him for a bit before a noise outside drove him to the doors so he could check it out.

Somewhere on the beach was Declan, no doubt having had a few Espen fans asking for his autograph. If he was down there enough, he was going to get more and more attention. Once word spread that he frequented this beach, fans would turn up to interact with him.

I got to see him in action yesterday. He was kind and courteous to every person who came up to him. I noticed how it eventually started to wear on him, but he never dropped his smile nor made anyone feel like he didn't have time for them. He was welcomed to Espen by the fans with open arms. It further solidified what I already knew about the city I played for and loved. It was the best place in the world.

Chapter 11

Declan

Brock was gay.

The one thing I always wanted to be reality. Even through the tinted windows I knew Brock watched me. I made sure to look back, let him see I knew he was there. Under normal circumstances, I wouldn't push someone who didn't want me. That shit was just fucked up. But when I stood in front of Brock, I saw something in his eyes, something he tried to hide from me.

Brock wanted me. That wasn't my ego talking. It was what I could see in his face. Why he fought it so hard made no sense to me. Maybe it wasn't the smartest move to start with the *let's fuck* line. Brock wasn't the kind of guy who wanted some random hookup. He was the type to want a partner. Someone by his side.

Why couldn't that someone be me?

I'd spent so many years settling for friends with benefits or the person you take home once or twice, but never actually date. Probably why the *let's have fun* shit was the first thing to come out of my mouth. Stupid. Too bad there wasn't a way to rewind time. Get a do over. Even with my mistake, I wasn't giving up.

Brock could say it wasn't a good idea all he wanted. I knew he didn't mean it. It was right there in his eyes. He was kind, not a liar. If he didn't really want me, he would have said so from the beginning. Those words never left his mouth, which had me wondering exactly what the reason might be.

There were a few people still milling around the beach. Most of them ignored me, focused on their walks along the water as the sun started to descend. The pinks and purples reflecting off the surface of the water were beautiful. There was nothing like it in my house in Maryland. I stayed and watched the sun fall below the horizon.

It gave Brock time to regroup. He obviously hadn't meant for me to hear the conversation. At thirty-two, only two, well now three people knew he was gay. What kind of existence could that be? Constantly hiding who you were from everyone. I'd been honest with my family from the beginning. When it came to baseball, I hadn't hidden my sexuality, I just hadn't made any big announcements. Then, Callen Teague came out to the world and being a gay or bi baseball player didn't matter anymore. I had a feeling that football was a completely different animal.

With the sun down, I went back to the house, but Brock was nowhere to be found. A note sat on the kitchen counter.

There's a plate of salmon and roasted vegetables in the fridge from lunch if you're hungry. I wasn't feeling well so I went to bed.

Brock

Giving him some time alone had been the right call. I couldn't give him too much, though. I'd wanted Brock in some way, shape, or form for more than ten years. I wouldn't give up when I knew there was a real possibility of an us.

After heating up the plate Brock left, I finished every bite and placed the dish in the dishwasher. Everything he cooked tasted like it was gourmet. Definitely on the level of the steak I had earlier for lunch. I climbed the stairs, stopping outside of Brock's closed door. I wondered if he actually went to sleep this early or if he was just lying in the dark, willing his eyes to close and his mind to stop.

Or maybe I was worried that would be me in a little bit. It was still pretty early but playing video games didn't interest me at the moment. I forced myself to leave Brock's door and go into my own room. With the door shut, I stripped off the shorts I put on for my trek to the beach and wandered into the bathroom. I flicked on the shower and finished stripping while I waited for the steam to fill the room.

No way would I be able to go to bed with the sticky salt air still clinging to my skin. With the water as hot as I could stand it, I rinsed away the sand and the sweat, watching the water swirl down the drain, Brock the sole focus of my thoughts.

How could I get past the wall Brock had obviously built around himself and his heart? It seemed insurmountable.

I only had a few days before my first away series with the Emperors, which didn't leave me with much time.

I stepped out of the shower and toweled off, dropping it into the hamper on the way by. Slipping on a pair of boxers, I lay down on top of the covers and picked up the book I'd been reading from the nightstand. If there was anything that could help clear my head so I could sleep, it was the murder mystery that had kept me up later than need be a few nights in a row.

After the sixth time reading the same paragraph, I closed the book and let it drop to my side. Apparently, Brock's earlier revelations were too much even for a book I'd been captivated with from the beginning.

I dropped my arm over my eyes. A plan. I needed a plan. Until I figured out a way to get Brock, I'd never have another night of decent sleep. My semi-hard cock was completely agreeing with that statement. Tempted beyond reason to wander back down the hall.

Temptation.

That was it. I needed to be pure, unadulterated temptation. The kind no sane man could resist. That moment of desire I saw in his eyes was unguarded. A crack in the wall. I just needed to find a way to make the crack wider so I could make a path through it and show Brock why he should let the whole thing fall.

That crack, the one where he watched me, bright-eyed and curious, I wanted to see that look again. Only this time, I wouldn't give him a chance to hide it from me. This time, he wouldn't be able to resist.

***

The plan to get Brock part one started this morning. I'd set my alarm to get up earlier than usual. Brock liked to work out first thing in the morning, and I planned on being in his home gym all hot and sweaty before he even walked in. I snuck quietly down the stairs, hoping Sampson would be too deep in puppy dreams in Brock's room to hear me. That or he'd ignore me.

When I reached the gym, without hearing sounds of Brock stirring, I blew out a breath. Now, it was time to get sweaty. Normally, I'd wait to work out in the stadium gym, but this was for a good cause. Two workouts in one day wouldn't hurt me. I'd go much lighter before the game.

I made sure to start with the stationary bike, getting my heart rate up without being too rough on my knees. Then I moved onto the weights, all while listening for sounds of Brock in the house. For the first time, I worked out with nothing but the sound of my breathing. Definitely a unique experience for me.

Sampson's nails clicked on the floor, and I knew Brock was heading this way. In the moment, what I was doing seemed childish. Then I remembered that brief second the night before. It had to be worth it in the end. I brought two kettlebells over, one on each side and started with a deadlift. Oh, and I made sure my ass faced the door while I bent over to lift them off the floor.

I wrapped my hands around the handles and waited.

"Damn." The whispered word carried across the room to me.

Thank god for the mirrored wall in the gym to watch your form. Only, I wasn't watching it. Instead, I moved my gaze up to Brock's eyes where they were focused firmly on my ass. I made sure to do a few reps before standing and turning to face Brock.

His cheeks were slightly pink, and he shifted from foot to foot, clearly flustered at finding me in the gym when he expected to be alone.

"I didn't think you were up," he said, still standing in the doorway.

I took the kettlebells over to the shelf. "Figured I'd get an early start."

He threw his thumb over his shoulder. "I... uh... I'll come back when you're done."

"Don't be ridiculous. You have plenty of equipment for us both to work out."

Brock shook his head, taking half a step back. "No. It's okay. I don't want to be in your way."

"You're not going to be in my way." I walked over and laid my hand on his shoulder, guiding him into the room. "I'm used to working out with a ton of people around, watching."

"But—"

"No, buts. This is your house. You don't have to change your workout routine for me. I'll stay over here, out of your way." I moved to the weight rack. "If I'm in your way, just tell me, and I'll change to another exercise."

Brock opened his mouth to argue, but I figured he realized he ran out of excuses to give me. He had no choice except to stay and work out with me. At least we were both going to pretend to work out. Reality was, I focused on getting Brock to watch me, not really paying attention to reps and form, while Brock tried his hardest to keep his focus on the exercise and not me.

I may have cheated a little bit when I noticed him finish an entire rep set without looking over. Somehow, he'd found a way to ignore me and that just wouldn't do. I tugged my tank top over my head and used it to wipe the sweat from my brow. Whether he realized it or not, Brock's gaze lingered on the V at my waist.

All the work I'd done to get those six-pack abs had been worth it. His hand started to shake holding the weight. He hadn't thrown me out of the room or stormed off yet, which meant I could push him just a little bit more for the day. I stepped over and ran my fingers down his forearm to his hand, helping to hold the weight.

"Cramp?" I asked, trying to keep my voice clear and innocent.

If my touch was affecting Brock even half as much as it was me, I knew his brain was scrambling for blood to answer the question.

"Huh?"

I used my other hand to take his fingers off the weight and placed it on the rack. Before Brock could utter a word of protest, I took his hand in both of mine and gently began massaging it.

A husky sigh left his lips, which seemed to bring Brock's focus back. He practically yanked his hand from mine. "What are you doing?" He wasn't angry, just curious and a little shocked.

I pointed to the hand he held to his chest. "Massaging out the cramp. Happens to us all the time from the glove and catching. The team docs know great massages and pressure points to work the pain out. Give me your hand. It'll feel better in no time."

Brock scooted back around the weight bench, out of my reach. "No, it's fine. I don't need you to do that. Actually, I think I just need a shower and a bottle of water."

Brock bolted from the room. On the floor near the weight bench sat his half empty bottle of water. I smirked while I put the room back in order and collected the water bottles and dirty towels.

Seemed like step one of my plan worked, otherwise Brock wouldn't have run. I'd give him a bit more space for the rest of the day.

Tomorrow, it was time for step two.

Chapter 12

Brock

Declan was down in Maryland for an away series against the Backfins. It was his first time playing his old team. He was happy before he left, saying how his old teammates invited him and some of the Emperors out to dinner tonight. It was nice that they were getting together, even though I was sure not everyone got along well.

Last night, I stayed home and watched the game. The Backfins won by three. It sucked seeing the Emperors lose, but I was hopeful they'd get the win tonight and tomorrow night.

In the short time Declan had been here, I'd gotten used to having him around, even if he wasn't here twenty-four seven. Having him gone last night felt off. I'd lived here alone since I'd bought it, yet the house felt alive with Declan here.

My thoughts drifted back to finding him in my workout room, all glistening with sweat. It was all I could do not to grip myself and relieve the ache that built at the sight. I was drawn into the room and soon after, he massaged my hand. He might as well have been stroking my dick for the way his fingers felt on me.

I had to get out of there before I came in my shorts, which wouldn't have been embarrassing at all. I'd never had a hands-free orgasm, but it was brewing right below the surface as he was working the pressure points in my hand.

Using the excuse I needed water, I fled to my bedroom. As soon as the door was shut behind me, I leaned heavily against it and stroked myself to an intense climax. I had to bite my fist to keep from calling out his name. Because that was exactly who I was thinking about. Declan with his lips pressed against the pulse point in my neck while his hand worked me over good.

I groaned and palmed myself where I sat on the couch. I'd already jerked off twice today: once when I got up and again after breakfast.

Something triggered in me when he touched my hand. Since then, I'd gotten off more times than I usually did in a week. Plus, knowing he would gladly fool around with me, it was more than I could bear.

But I'd stayed solid in my resolve. I hadn't given in to him saying we could be more. Not more. That was the wrong word. There was no promise of a relationship. It was merely fooling around. Having some fun. I didn't want to have fun, though. Even if I hadn't made the promise to Ethan, I still wouldn't be satisfied with fun.

In my fantasies, I saw Declan when he came. How he'd look with my dick deep inside him. How he'd hold me tight as he pounded into me. I was itching to know if he'd look that way in real life.

Did he top? Bottom? Switch?

Usually when I met men for a hookup, they assumed I topped. And I would do so gladly, but I also wanted to try bottoming. I'd never done it before. Never trusted someone to take enough care of me. It was a very vulnerable position to be in.

My phone ringing startled me. Looking down, I realized I had my dick out and was stroking it. I seriously needed to get a grip on my libido. It was out of control.

Tucking myself back into my shorts, I glanced at my phone and saw Ethan's name. Well, if something was going to kill the moment, he was it.

"How's it going?" I said, answering the phone.

Ethan and I talked on a semi-regular basis. Most of the time it was texting but with Declan living with me, the calls had been more frequent, usually when Ethan knew Declan was playing a game and not here.

"Good. How are you?"

"Fine." What was the point of this small talk when the real reason he called was to check in on his brother? "He's doing good, Ethan."

He blew out a breath. "I'm glad. I wasn't sure how he'd be going back to Maryland."

"You could have called him and asked him yourself."

"Yeah, but then he'd accuse me of checking in too often."

"Which is exactly what you're doing."

"He doesn't need to know it, unless you're telling him."

I sighed. "Ethan, I have zero desire to be in the middle of anything between you and Dec. And honestly, as much as I love you like a brother, you can't keep doing this. You'll drive yourself crazy. He's a grown man. I'm not keeping tabs on him. When he's here, he's happy. I don't know what he does outside of here, though."

"I wouldn't ask you to find out."

"Good, because I wouldn't do it." I took a calming breath, trying to understand Ethan's side of things. I did get it, both of their sides, but I was being honest when I said I didn't want to be in the middle of the two of them and that's exactly where I was. "Listen, if anything truly was the matter, I'd tell you. But he's fine. Now go back to your life and chill out. I got your brother's back."

"You have no idea how reassuring it is to know you're there for Declan since I can't be." If he only knew just how *there for Declan* I wanted to be.

"At some point, you're going to have to let this go. I don't know when that will be, but it's not healthy for your relationship with him."

"Has he said something to you?" I could hear the slight panic in his voice. Ethan's heart was in the right place, but he could be too overbearing and all that did was chase Declan away.

"No." I hated lying to Ethan. It wasn't that Declan went around the house complaining about his brother all the time, but when Ethan checked in, Declan would gripe for a bit. When did my loyalty start to shift from wanting to do what I could for Ethan to trying to keep Declan's life private from his brother?

I loved my brother, but if I behaved like Ethan, he'd tell me exactly what I could do with my incessant checking in.

Ethan changed the subject and before I knew it, a half hour had gone by before we hung up. I started walking around the living area, all this pent-up energy inside me trying to break free. I was lying to my best friend. He didn't ask if Declan had come on to me. He wouldn't. There was no reason to think so. And my promise to Ethan remained intact. But it was so tempting to give in to Declan when he was here. When he encompassed all of my senses.

I hated to admit it, but I missed Declan.

Then I got an idea.

I sent a quick text off to Lali and asked her if she'd like a furry houseguest for the night, to which she readily agreed. Then I texted Declan. It was early yet. The game wasn't scheduled until tonight.

Me: What hotel are you staying at?

Declan: The Hilton down the street from the stadium. Why?

Me: Want a visitor?

In the back of my mind was a voice whispering just how stupid this was, but I didn't care. I missed Declan. No matter how much it would tempt me to be in his presence, it was better than sitting at home with my dick in my hand, thinking about the man I couldn't have.

Declan: Hell, yeah! Get down here. I'll make sure there's a ticket for you at the window for tonight's game.

Me: That would be great. It will be the first time I've seen you play in person in a while.

Declan: I'll be sure to be on top of my game tonight. *wink emoji*

Me: I hope I can get a room.

Declan: Leave it to me. I'll take care of it and text you.

Me: Thank you for doing that.

This was so bad. So stupid and yet I couldn't help myself.

With my plan in place, I went up to my room to pack a small duffle bag with clothes for tonight and tomorrow. I'd head back here sometime in the morning to miss the afternoon traffic of people driving home from the weekend.

Once I got my stuff and Sampson's loaded in the back of my Sequoia, I drove into the city to Lali's condo and dropped off my dog. Lali asked where I was going. I didn't lie, there was no point. She'd see right through me anyway. Lucky for me, she didn't say anything about me driving to Maryland to visit Declan, though I did get a knowing wink.

Back in my SUV heading south, I gave my mind over to the thoughts running rampant there. It was the one space I allowed myself to think of what it would be like to get my hands on Declan. The one space where I could do what I wanted.

By the time I was pulling up to the hotel, I was more than ready to get out of my SUV. The drive wasn't long, but my body didn't like being stuck in the same position for any stretch of time. The years of playing football made me feel like I was eighty not thirty-two.

I was walking through the hotel lobby with my bag in hand when someone came over to me.

The guy was in his mid-forties, if I had to guess. He had his son with him who had to be at least thirteen. His eyes were wide as he peered up at me.

"You're Brock Richmond," the dad said.

I was frozen in place. How did someone in Maryland recognize me when I was hardly recognized in the city I used to play in? I smiled. I wasn't one to soak up attention from the fans. Of course, I didn't get nearly as much as the quarterback on the team did. Or as much as Declan did down on the beach.

"I am."

He stuck out his hand. "It's great to meet you." I took it and shook. "I can't believe this. I've been a fan of the Sandpipers for years." I quirked an eyebrow. "I know, I know, the team wasn't great for a while but I'm a diehard fan. The new owners have already started to turn them around."

I nodded. "They have." Being a Sandpiper wasn't something I hated. The team wasn't great. Their record was terrible before it was bought. But I was still paid well and therefore gave it my all when I was on the field. I knew they were going to get better with each season under the new owners.

"Would you sign my son's hat?"

I glanced down to the boy and noticed the Backfins hat he was wearing. "You want me to sign that?"

He chuckled. "It's all we've got on us. I didn't expect to run into a Sandpipers player here."

I laughed. I was about to tell him I was just here to catch a game, although he didn't need to know that. Taking the black marker the guy held out, I scrawled my signature on the brim of the hat.

The boy held it in his hands then looked up at me with a big smile. "Thank you so much."

"You're welcome."

"It was great meeting you," the dad said. "You seriously made our day."

"Mine, too. Take care now."

"Bye!" the boy called back as they walked away.

After that, I was riding high as I checked in, made sure they billed me, not Declan, and eventually made my way to the stadium. It was nice to be noticed occasionally.

The game was one of those where everyone was on the edge of their seats. It wasn't a playoff or anything, but Ayden Thompson was one batter away from a no-hitter. His pitch count was low. There was no need to pull him from the game. Even the Backfins fans seemed to be holding their breaths. No-hitters were more common than perfect games; however, they still weren't an everyday occurrence.

I sat there with my hands white knuckling the seat. Emperors' fans were scattered throughout the stadium cheering their team. I worried if I blinked at the wrong time, I'd miss it.

But then it happened. Thompson got his first no-hitter of the season.

I jumped to my feet and cheered along with the other fans. Players on the Emperors came from the dugout. It didn't take me long to find Declan as he ran up to embrace his friend. I was really glad I drove down here for this.

When things calmed down and the game was over, I followed the rest of the fans out of the stadium. The walk to the hotel wasn't far. Luckily, there were a few in the area. I paid a lot more than I wanted to but was grateful to be in the same place as Declan.

Back in my room, I texted him my congratulations.

Declan: What room are you in?

Me: 322.

Declan: Stay put. I'll be there as soon as I can.

It was late. I was sure Declan wanted to celebrate with his friends, but I wasn't going anywhere. I came here to see him and that was what I would do.

A little over an hour ticked by before there was a knock on my door. When I opened it, Declan was there in his freshly showered glory. What I wouldn't give to tug him into my arms and hold him close. Inhale that scent of his which sped up my pulse.

I didn't have to wish for it. A second later, Declan pulled me in for a hug. "It's so great you're here." He pulled back with a big smile.

Reluctantly, I let him go and went farther into the room. Declan let the door close behind him. "That was an amazing game. Thompson was on fire."

"Hell yeah, he was."

"No celebrating tonight?"

"Nah, we all had drinks last night. Plus, Rome came down to watch Ayden for the series. He'd never been here and wanted to see the sights while Ayden was at the stadium during the day. He was waiting for Ayden when we left. What a great game for him to see."

I chuckled and could only imagine there would be no prying the two of them apart. "Hungry?"

"Yes, let's order room service."

"We could go out." I was sure there was still a lot open nearby with the game having just gotten over. Not everyone would be in a rush to get back to their homes and hotels on a Saturday night.

"Nah, let's stay in. I've done enough peopling for the day."

Declan and I browsed the menu and ordered food fit for six. We hung out well into the night talking about nothing, yet it felt like everything. Not once did he come on to me, push me for the fun he wanted to have, but I didn't miss the interest in his eyes. He didn't have to voice it for me to see it was still there. And what better place to give in than a hotel?

But I didn't. We eventually said goodnight and agreed to meet up before I got on the road tomorrow. I was glad I took the chance and came down here for the game.

Chapter 13

Declan

"What time will you be home?" The sound of Sampson's nails on the hardwood reached me through the phone. He was never more than a few feet from Brock, unless Sampson was being petted by someone else. I'd convinced Brock to call me when he got home. He swore that leaving early would have him missing most of the traffic, but I wanted to hear he'd gotten there in a reasonable amount of time.

"The game will probably end around four unless it goes into extra innings." I shoved my clothes into my bag and glanced around to make sure I hadn't missed anything. "We should be home around six-thirty."

What Brock didn't know was that I already had plans for us for the evening. Things were so comfortable between the two of us the night before. Sitting on the couch, having dinner, and watching TV. Much the same like we did at home, but there had been a difference in Brock. One I don't think he wanted me to notice.

He'd come to Maryland to watch me play when he could have seen me at any point since I arrived in Espen. So why did he come here? And why did I catch him staring at me every so often when he thought I wasn't looking?

The answer had hit me long after I went back to my room while I laid there, staring at the ceiling, trying to get some sleep. Brock wanted more than a quick fuck from whoever he dated. He was looking for forever, not just someone to date, which I was more than willing to give him. I'd known from the moment I'd suggested having fun together I'd made a mistake. A mistake I probably continued pushing when Brock found me in his workout room, drenched in sweat, and doing everything in my power to get him to stare at my ass. Hell, I would have been thrilled had he wanted to touch it.

Not only had he not touched my ass, but he ran like his was on fire. I knew I needed a new plan if I was going to get Brock. The only thing I kept coming back to was the tried-and-true method of romance. No man or woman could resist when someone tried to sweep them off their feet.

"What should we have for dinner? I can have it ready when you get here."

"Let me worry about dinner tonight." Someone knocked on the door. "Brock, I gotta go. Marcus is here. I'll see you later." Before Brock could protest or ask any more questions, I hung up and pulled my bag up onto my shoulder.

I tugged the door open and was surprised to see Ayden standing there. "Didn't expect to see you here this morning. Figured you'd be with Rome until the last possible moment."

"He wanted to get a jumpstart on sightseeing before he went home. There were a few things he said he still wanted to see. Since we'll be home tonight, there didn't seem to be a point to him hanging around, waiting for me to get done, when we have to take the bus home."

"Good point. I'm glad my first away series was short. Not like when we have to leave next week." I shut the door behind me and followed Ayden to the elevator.

"I bet you're relieved." The elevator doors closed behind us. "With that smile on your face, I'd be willing to bet you already found someone to hook up with in Espen."

Damn, was Ayden right on the money, but I couldn't say anything about who it might be. Brock had only told three people he was gay, including me, and it wasn't my right to oust him.

"I might have. I think it could be more than friends with benefits this time."

The corner of Ayden's mouth tilted up. "So, the self-proclaimed bachelor might have found someone to tame him."

"Maybe." I shrugged, playing it off. I didn't think I was ready until recently to admit it, but deep down I compared every single man or woman to Brock. It wasn't conscious on my part. Looking back on each of the people I tried dating, I could see every one of the traits I wanted in the person and left them when they didn't have something Brock did. I thought the teenage crush was just that. Apparently, my feelings for Brock ran deeper than even I recognized. "We'll have to see how tonight goes."

"Good luck." The elevator doors opened, and we walked out toward the shuttle to take us to the stadium.

***

The bus pulled into the Emperors' parking lot around seven-thirty. I hadn't really expected us to go three extra innings. It could have been worse. In the end, we took the series with two games. Did I feel a little bad beating my former team? Sure. They used to be my teammates. Now, the Emperors were, and I needed to celebrate and enjoy our wins.

I climbed off the shuttle and was happy to see everyone grab their stuff and scatter toward their cars with a wave. One thing was the same here and in Maryland—when you got back from being on the road, you just wanted to get home. No hanging out after an away series.

The employees of the stadium would unload our equipment truck when it arrived for our next game. We had one home series, then we were back on the road for a little over a week. Joe would expect us at the stadium early before the next game to review our plays, but until then I was free.

Before I left the lot, I called and ordered a takeout meal to pick up on my way back to Brock's. Not as romantic as cooking, but it was better than spending the night in the ER with food poisoning. Cooking had never been my specialty. My dad and brother were amazing cooks. My mom and I didn't inherit that gene.

The trip home was quick, even with the stop for dinner and a bottle of wine. I hadn't seen Brock drink much since I'd moved in, so I wasn't sure if he did drink. To me, every steak needed a good bottle of red with it.

I pulled into the garage, leaving my overnight bag in the car. I'd get it in the morning. Dinner and a movie were more important at the moment. With the bottle of wine under one arm and the bag of food in the other hand, I shut the garage door and walked up to the front door.

Brock's scent hit me as soon as I stepped inside. Being gone for a few days, it surrounded me right away like a warm blanket. A clean, woodsy scent I wished I could rub all over myself. Or that he'd rub all over me as we buried ourselves deep within each other's bodies.

I shook my head. I was getting ahead of myself. There was wining and dining to do first.

"Brock?" I called out on my way to the kitchen. Sampson came barreling around the corner. I set the bottle and bag on the counter before squatting down to scratch behind his ears.

"You're back. Congrats on the win. Sorry about the extra innings." Brock came down the stairs looking hot as hell. I had to stand up as the blood flowed from my brain straight to my cock. No need to get dizzy and fall over trying to keep my balance.

"Thanks. It happens. I hoped to get back sooner than this."

"Well, you're here now."

His shirt was tight in his shoulders but a little looser around his waist. After seeing him on the beach with a shirt on every time, I had a feeling Brock was self-conscious about his body. I really didn't think he knew just how sexy he was. He didn't need a V to turn me on. He did it with the scruff around his mouth and his broad shoulders.

I reached into the bag and started to unload the takeout containers, which were a black plastic. Much nicer than the Styrofoam containers I was used to. Hopefully, it kept the steaks as juicy as they were in the restaurant.

"I'm not much of a cook, so I figured this was the safer option."

Brock walked over to the counter. "You didn't have to pick up dinner. I could have made something."

"You cook every night. I wanted to do something nice for you."

His eyes widened. "For me? Why?"

"Why?" I opened the containers and started dishing the food onto plates. "Because you let me stay here. You drove down to Maryland to watch me play. You could have seen me play in Espen, but you knew, as happy as I was to see my old team, it would be hard to play against them and beat them."

A light pink tinted his cheeks. "I wanted to see you and make sure you were okay."

I reached out and covered his hand where it rested on the counter. "And I appreciate that more than you know."

I expected him to move his hand and I was pleasantly surprised when he didn't. "You're welcome."

Our eyes stayed connected for a few moments longer and I could feel the shift. The subtle change in the way Brock looked at me. He darted his eyes away like he was fighting with himself.

I didn't want him to be nervous or unsure, so I changed the subject and held up the bottle of wine. "Every steak needs a good glass of red." I raised a brow and waited for him.

"It does." Brock nodded and moved around the counter to pull two wine glasses from one of the cabinets.

"How about a movie with dinner?" I asked, uncorking the bottle and filling the two glasses.

Brock pulled out two serving trays and loaded our plates onto them. "I like that idea."

I carried the glasses of wine to the coffee table in the living room and came back for one of the trays, which now had our plates, silverware, and napkins on them.

Settled on the couch, we searched through the different streaming stations until we found a movie we both wanted to watch. Honestly, Brock could have put on anything he wanted. The movie didn't matter to me. I was more interested in the company than the TV.

With empty plates and glasses, I noticed we'd shifted to sit closer to one another as the movie progressed. The night before in my hotel room had a different feel to it than this moment. That was laughter and camaraderie. This was intimacy and closeness. Something I hoped to have more of.

I turned my head toward Brock on the couch. "Thanks for letting me stay and thanks for having dinner with me tonight. This was nice."

Brock's cheeks were a bit flushed from the wine or the tension between us. Who knew? I watched his eyes dart down to my mouth. We were on the same wavelength. It seemed I wanted his lips on mine as badly as he wanted mine on his. I couldn't make the first move this time. He'd been clear about that not happening between us the first night I suggested it. I was more than willing to convince him otherwise. I just wasn't willing to be the first, in case he still didn't want that.

His lids lowered slightly and he leaned in. When he stopped, I thought he changed his mind. I figured he'd pull back, make up some excuse for his behavior, then dart upstairs.

But then his lips touched mine and I ceased to think about the what-ifs. I didn't know if this was going to be my only kiss with Brock. Just in case, I wanted to taste every inch of him.

I leaned in to his lips and slid my hand behind his neck, holding his mouth to mine. I didn't want to give him a moment to worry about whether we should or shouldn't be doing this and ran my tongue along his bottom lip. It parted slightly and I wasted no time slipping my tongue into his mouth and getting my first taste of Brock.

And what a taste it was.

Chapter 14

Brock

Normally, lying in bed wasn't my thing. Once I was awake, I was up. This morning, I didn't want to move. I'd lain here for an hour so far. Declan had a game tonight, so he'd be heading to the stadium at some point.

I felt myself getting hard as I thought back to what happened last night. What shouldn't have happened. I'd like to blame it on the wine since I rarely drank, but one glass for a man my size wouldn't knock me on my ass. It did, however, make me do something I was valiantly fighting against up until then.

The way his lips felt against mine, I never wanted it to end. I was starting to push him backward against the cushions so I could line my body up with his. I wanted to see if he was as hard as I was. Wanted to know what it felt like to slide my dick alongside his. I didn't care that we were clothed. I was willing to take whatever I could get.

Then reality slammed into me, and I slowly retreated. It was sheer torture to do so. Fortunately, Declan didn't appear upset. He simply sat up, brushed his lips once more against mine, and we went back to watching the movie.

We cleaned up our dishes afterward, while Sampson made one last trip outside for the night. Declan and I climbed the stairs together with Sampson on our heels. We didn't kiss again but Declan did touch his fingers to mine when he said goodnight.

I jerked off twice before I was finally able to get my body to calm down enough to pass out. At least I got some sleep. Now I was wide awake.

Sampson walked over to nudge me with his snout. It was past the time he normally went out. After going to the bathroom and brushing my teeth, my dick was no longer hard as steel, and I was able to walk downstairs without my desire for Declan evident.

Since his bedroom door was open, I knew he was already up. I expected to find him in the kitchen but there was nothing except a freshly brewed pot of coffee. Glancing to the sliding doors, I saw him lounging in one of the chairs on the deck. The sun was shining, only a few clouds in the sky. Sampson danced near the door when I approached. As soon as I slid it open, he gave Declan a happy sniff and tail wag before going down the stairs to take care of business. I closed the door behind me, not wanting the cool air inside the house to escape.

A clothed Declan was hard enough to resist. Him without a shirt on was nearly impossible. All those muscles on display. His shorts low on his hips. My mouth watered, last night flashing in my mind. I wanted to climb on top of him. Get up close and personal with his flawless skin.

He tipped his head back to smile at me where I still stood in the same place I stopped when I came outside. I was rendered stupid at his good looks. "Good morning."

I cleared my throat and moved forward to the railing, so he was at my back and couldn't see how my dick was attempting to vie for his attention. "Morning." I should say something more. Something to address what we did last night. But I refused to tell him we shouldn't have done that. It was the truth; however, I didn't want Declan to feel like me kissing him was a mistake. It was more of a lapse in judgment.

"Things don't have to be weird between us because of last night," he said. Well, at least one of us had the balls to speak up.

"It's not weird."

I heard him get up from the chair, his mug being set down on the small table beside it. He placed his hand on the small of my back for a brief moment before he moved to stand next to me, angling his body in my direction. My eyes were drawn to his. He was simply stunning out here in the warm light of morning.

He smiled. "It is a little."

I blew out a breath. "I'm sorry. I'm not good at this, not that I know what this is. I just... I haven't been with anyone in a while. Well, we're not *with* each other. All we did was kiss. But that kiss... And this morning... I'm not sure—"

He laid his hand on my arm. "Brock, stop."

Thirty-two years old and I couldn't get myself together. "I'm sorry."

"You don't have to apologize." The gentleness in his tone eased my nervousness a little. "We don't have to talk about this or anything else until you're ready. I'm not going anywhere."

"Thank you. I just..."

"You need time to think."

I nodded.

Declan reached into his pocket and retrieved his phone. He shook his head with a smirk.

"What is it?"

"Ethan's in a 'check on Declan' instead of a 'check in with Declan' kind of mood today."

Now it was my turn to shake my head. "He needs to find someone and settle down with them. He has too much time on his hands."

"You'd think his job would keep him busy." Declan laughed. He turned to go into the house. "I'm going to grab a quick bite then get ready to head to the stadium."

"Dec?" Stopping, he peered at me over his shoulder. "I get that he's too overprotective and it drives you crazy, but he does it from a place of love. You're the only brother he has."

Declan offered me a small smile. "I know. I'm not sure what I'd do without him. When we really talk to each other, I miss him even more. I just wish that one out of every three conversations I have with my brother didn't include questions that should come from my parents. When you call Wyatt, do you talk about his life in college or his car payments?"

I shrugged. "Always about his life."

"That's how it should be. Ethan and I have that ninety-nine percent of the time. I'd love to have that last one percent, too."

"Then tell him that."

Declan paused for a moment. "You're right. I need to talk to him. I'm still ignoring him for now, though."

"Great." I rolled my eyes. "He'll text me since you're not responding."

Declan's laugh was like music to my ears as he retreated into the house. It was hard playing devil's advocate. I felt for both of them. Ethan wasn't a bad guy, he just needed to calm down and get a freaking life. If he texted me, I was going to tell him he needed to get laid and leave it at that.

For the next hour, I waited for his text, but thankfully nothing came through. Guilt started to eat away at me thinking of my best friend. I kissed his brother. I did exactly what I promised I wouldn't do. And I was the one who initiated it. Not only would I have to act like everything was normal next time I was on the phone with Ethan, but I had to continue to leave out to Declan what his brother said to me. My life was turning into a TV drama. All I needed now was for Reed to show up and tell me he was pregnant with my baby.

I shook that image from my head.

Declan got ready and left for the stadium. They had a game tonight. He would only be home for these three games then he'd be on the road again. It reaffirmed how right my decision was to retire. I loved being home.

With the earlier mention of my brother, I decided to send him a text to see if he was busy. I had no idea what his schedule was but hopefully he was free. I had the urge to talk to him.

My phone rang after I sent the text and Wyatt's name popped up on the screen.

"Hey, how are you?" I asked when I answered.

"I'm good. Better now that I've graduated."

I chuckled. "I bet. You worked hard. You deserve the break."

"I do. I might bother you for a spare room for a week or two over the summer."

"You know you're welcome here any time."

"How's it going living with Declan?" Of course, my parents told him. Not that I thought they wouldn't.

"Good. Between home games and being on the road, he's not here more than he is."

"Has he had any luck finding a new place?" That was a good question and one I hadn't brought up to Declan. I liked having him here. No, I loved it. If I asked him about it, I was worried he'd think I was trying to push him out of my house. So, I kept my lips shut on the subject.

"He's been busy getting situated with the Emperors." That was one way to avoid answering the question.

"I imagine it's not easy going from team to team." I was lucky that I was with the Sandpipers for the length of my career with the NFL. "I doubt you called me to talk about Declan, though." Wyatt saw right through me.

"Ethan had texted Dec and it reminded me I hadn't spoken to you in a while."

He chuckled. "Is Ethan still the overprotective brother?"

"Mmhmm."

"I'm so glad you're not that way."

"Our relationship was never like that."

"No, it wasn't. How are you doing? Anything new?" Whenever I talked to Wyatt, we mostly spoke about him. My life was boring outside of football. Unless Wyatt wanted to hear stories about Sampson chasing crabs on the beach or which new guy Lali was dating, I didn't have much to say on my end.

Instead of going through the usual conversation we had when we talked, I said, "I have something I want to tell you." When I told Declan I was gay, after he overheard it, it was like something unlocked in me. Now I wanted Wyatt to know.

"You can say anything to me, and I won't breathe it to anyone nor would I ever judge you." That was my brother. He was so open and caring. He had a heart of gold. But how was he going to handle what I was about to say?

"I... Shit."

"This must be big if you're cursing." I could hear the humor in his voice.

My palms were sweating, my heart was racing. I had to do this. "I'm gay, Wyatt."

Nothing. Utter silence.

"Wyatt?"

"Sorry! I'm here. A little stunned, but here. Is this a new revelation or something you've always been?"

"I've known I was gay since I was in my early teens or about there. I'm sorry I didn't tell you sooner. I wasn't sure how anyone was going to react then everything happened with football, and I didn't want to jeopardize—"

"Brock, stop." Those were the same words Declan said to me earlier. I needed to get my nervous rambling under control. I heard Wyatt take a breath. "You don't have to explain to me why you didn't tell me sooner. It's not my business. But I'm glad you told me now."

My voice was small and so unlike me. "I don't have to hide anymore."

"No, you don't. You should never have had to hide who you truly are and I'm sorry you felt that way. Please know that no matter what, I'll never turn my back on you. If anything, I'll be your biggest supporter."

"I don't deserve you." My brother really was amazing.

"Since we're confessing... You're not the only one waving the rainbow flag, big brother."

It was my turn to be rendered speechless.

"Brock?"

"I gotta say, I never expected that to come out of your mouth."

He laughed. "I wasn't planning on telling you yet, but I couldn't let you take the leap alone."

"Now I know I don't deserve you. And I'll do the same and not inquire as to why you didn't tell me sooner. Just know that I love you, Wyatt."

"I love you, too." I could hear him sniffle on the other end of the line. My brother was always more sensitive than me. Kids used to pick on him in school about it. They didn't understand how much of a better person it made Wyatt. They had this macho ideal in their heads that boys weren't supposed to show emotion. Ridiculous.

"Do Mom and Dad know?"

"No, and I'm guessing they don't know about you either."

I shook my head, even though he couldn't see me. "Nope."

"Our next family dinner should be really fucking interesting." My brother was not like me in the sense that he swore freely.

There were a lot of differences between us. Where I was taller and broader, Wyatt was shorter than me at six foot even. He didn't inherit the body hair trait I did from my dad. I had a fuzzy chest and legs but not to the point of being too much. Wyatt wasn't broad but he did have lean muscles. His mode of exercise was laps in the pool at college. When he visited me, he was in the ocean a lot. I swore he was a fish in a previous life.

The one visible trait we shared was our eyes. They were exactly the same dark brown. His matched his hair almost perfectly where my hair was nearly black.

"At least we'll be a united front during that meal," I replied.

"Yeah, but I don't think we'll need to be. Mom and Dad aren't going to care. It's funny, actually, that neither of us spoke up before this."

"I don't know about you, but it was easier keeping it a secret."

"I didn't have time to explore it more. Sure, I've had hookups in college, but my education meant more to me than random dick."

"On that note, I think we've said enough."

Wyatt busted out laughing. "So, you're saying we shouldn't exchange stories when we see each other next?"

"Wyatt," I grumbled low.

He kept laughing. "Thanks for being the best brother in the world."

"Ditto, kid."

Chapter 15

Declan

Ships in the night.

That was what Brock and I seemed to be lately. Three night games in a row. By the time I got home from the stadium, Brock was either already in bed or heading up. I knew he watched the games. It was the only thing we talked about since the morning I told him I knew he needed time. When I said time, I thought a day, at most, two. Now here we were, three days later, and I had to catch a flight to the West Coast with the team later today.

Not for the first time, I wondered if he was avoiding me. Trying to find a way to rebuild his walls. It was one of my biggest fears about traveling for the next week. Without being in Brock's presence every day, I wondered whether it would be easier for him to convince himself that we shouldn't have kissed.

His lips on mine had set a fire in my blood. One I didn't want to extinguish. Seeing Brock every morning while we had coffee or breakfast only made me crave him more. I tried to find small ways to touch him, keep that constant connection, hoping it would make him see how good we could be together.

That was what I wanted more than anything. A relationship with Brock. More than just his hands on my body and his mouth devouring mine. I wanted the small connection between us to grow and get stronger. For that to happen, I needed Brock to see how great a relationship with me could be and be willing to give us a shot. Something we couldn't do while I was three thousand miles away.

I finished packing my suitcase and left my bedroom. It was light enough I could carry it down the stairs to leave it by the front door. I hadn't even left yet, and I couldn't wait to return home.

Home.

Wasn't that the bitch of it all? I kept calling this place home, but I hadn't bothered to look for one of my own.

A few people had walked through my place in Maryland. No bites so far. That didn't mean I couldn't start looking for somewhere to live until then. My realtor was sure it would sell sooner rather than later. So what was the hold up?

Every day off, I promised myself I'd go talk to a realtor here in Espen. I'd see what houses were for sale and visit a few of them. Each and every time I found myself unwilling to give up Brock's company to go in search of a house to live separately from him.

Living with Brock gave me the opportunity to see him all the time. To relax with him on my days off. To talk baseball, about Sampson, even our plans for the day. Everything was perfect as it was. Well, almost perfect. In my dream scenario, Brock and I shared a bed every night on top of our lives together.

I set my bag by the front door and found Brock's eyes dart from my suitcase to me from where he sat at the table working on his laptop.

"What time's your flight?"

"Not until four. Joe asked them to move it back two hours. After three night games, he wanted us to get some rest before we play in a different time zone. Since Saturday's a night game, it works."

"Good. Are you hungry? Do you want some lunch?"

"Lunch sounds great if you were making it for yourself. If not, don't worry about me. I can grab something on the way to the stadium."

Brock closed his laptop. "No, don't do that. I'm happy to whip something up. I need to eat, too."

He went to the fridge and started pulling out ingredients for who knew what. His laugh caught my attention. Deep and rich. Like a warm blanket on a cold night. "You really don't do much cooking, do you?"

I moved my gaze to his and silently begged my dick to keep itself under control. "No. Everything I tried to make came out burned and inedible. I'm more of a takeout guy. Tastes better and a whole lot better for my stomach."

"Ah, so you cook like your mom."

"Yep. And Ethan cooks like my dad. Too bad I didn't inherent Dad's gifts in the kitchen."

Brock picked up the knife and began chopping vegetables. "I remember your dad's meals when I was over for dinner. Always amazing."

"Dad is a pretty fantastic cook. What are you making?"

"Greek chicken salad with orzo."

"Sounds delicious."

Brock nodded and continued making lunch. The stilted conversation morphed into tension filled silence. I had to bite my tongue more than once to stop myself from asking him what he decided. The decision had to come from him, even if it was killing me waiting. These next nine days were going to suck.

Two away series. More than a week for Brock to talk himself out of doing anything else with me. To convince himself it had been a mistake. A product of the wine and nothing else. Somehow, I had to find a way to keep him from overthinking things. Keep me at the forefront of his mind, exactly where he was in mine.

Brock finished lunch and set the bowl in front of me. "Thank you. This looks great."

After that, I tried to draw Brock into a few different conversations, but they all seemed to fizzle out quickly. Like his mind was elsewhere. I didn't know how else to get him to talk to me. Things felt awkward. The simmering attraction between us was still there, but Brock kept me at arm's length.

Even though I didn't like it, and in the end, it could give Brock space to think of excuses about why we shouldn't be together, being apart could give the tension between us time to either come to a head and we could move forward or we could go back to where we were when I first moved in.

It would suck. I'd have to shove my attraction for Brock back into the box it had been in for years. I'd do it if it meant things would return to the way they were. Being together would be my first choice. I'd wanted him since I was a teenager. I just wasn't selfish or stupid enough to destroy our friendship over it if Brock didn't want the same thing.

I took a book out onto the patio while the time before I had to leave ticked away. Brock stayed inside on his laptop, letting Sampson out every so often. It felt like I blinked and had to leave for the stadium where the shuttle would be waiting to take us to the airport.

I shoved the book into my carry-on bag, double-checking to make sure I had everything I needed for the flight. A sound behind me caught my attention. When I glanced over my shoulder, Brock stood there with his hands in the pockets of his khaki shorts. Probably thought that was the safest place to keep them.

"Have a safe flight."

I stood, tugging my bag onto my shoulder, and turned to face Brock. "Thanks. Don't be too bored here without me." I tried to infuse a little humor. It was only a nine day away series, yet the finality of leaving weighed heavily on me. I may not know the outcome, but I did know that when I returned, the relationship I had with Brock would be forever changed.

"Thanks. I'll text you when I land."

"I'd like that." He tugged his hands from his pockets and held them up. "Not 'cause I'm checking up on you."

"I know." I turned to the door and grabbed the handle of my bag. I glanced over my shoulder. "I'll see you the Monday after next."

"Bye, Dec."

Brock waved as I closed the door and took the stairs down to the garage. When I reached the bottom and looked up, I saw Brock watching me from the window. I could have stopped. Could have waved.

My gut tightened. I dropped my head and kept moving toward my car. I tossed my bag into the trunk and climbed in the driver's side. Brock was still in the window when I backed out of the garage. This time, I couldn't resist and lifted my hand in a wave before driving away.

When I arrived in the lot, there were cars, luggage, players, and coaches everywhere. People giving their bags to the guys loading the shuttle. Longer away series and flights were always more chaotic than local games and bus rides.

I lined my bag up near the others and with my carry-on climbed on board the shuttle. Ayden had already flown out since he was the starter for the first game. He'd left on Wednesday night while we played. Marcus sat in one of the seats near the middle.

"Anyone sitting here?"

"Nope. Have at it."

I sat down next to Marcus. On bus rides to games, we each got our own set of two seats. For a quick shuttle ride to the airport, we squished on. I closed my eyes and leaned my head back.

"Already tired?"

I looked over at him. "Nah, I just hate the whole travel part. I'd rather be there already."

Marcus laughed. "Can't say I hate travel. Not when my husband owns an aviation company."

"You've got a point."

Joe stood at the front of the shuttle. "Everyone have everything they need?"

A chorus of yeses filled the plane while Dominic stood and saluted Joe. "Yes, sir."

Joe rolled his eyes and turned to the driver. "Let's go."

Within an hour we were boarded on the plane and ready to take off. I put my earbuds in and started the movie I'd downloaded onto my tablet.

The flight was smooth. Airline food never really did it for me and Brock's delicious lunch had long worn off by the time we collected our bags. Once we were on the bus, I sent Brock the text I promised.

Me: Here. Heading to the hotel now, then going to find dinner.

Brock: Didn't they feed you on the plane?

Me: Airplane food does not live up to your salad.

The bubbles appeared and disappeared multiple times before I gave up waiting and shoved the phone back into my pocket. Frustrated, I walked out into the cool night air in the direction of the bus to the hotel. Brock would talk when he was ready.

When we arrived at the hotel and checked in, I sent Ayden my room number and asked if he wanted to grab something to eat. I yanked my bag through the door and dumped my backpack onto the bed.

Seconds later, someone knocked and my stomach growled in appreciation that I was going to feed it. I opened the door.

"Did you forget to eat on the plane?"

"Shut up. You know that food sucks. Plus, I know your dumbass hasn't eaten, otherwise, you wouldn't be standing here. You'd be on a video call jerking off with Rome."

Ayden shrugged and laughed. "True. Let's go."

I shut the door behind me and followed Ayden to the elevator. "I'm fucking starving and ready to go home."

"Already? You just got here." The elevator doors closed behind us. "Does that mean you really did find someone?"

While I wanted to tell Ayden about Brock, there wasn't much for me to tell. We were still in this weird limbo with the walls Brock had put up the moment his lips separated from mine. And I didn't know how to get them down.

"It's complicated."

One of his brows lifted. "Complicated? You don't do complicated."

Wasn't that the truth. The benefit of one-night stands and friends with benefits meant no strings. No hoops to jump through. Brock was different. I'd jump through hoops covered in gasoline and set on fire if it meant I could wake up every morning with him by my side. "It seems like now I do. I really think this guy is worth it."

"Oh so, it's a guy this time. Well, let me be the first to say, welcome to the Emperors' gay baseball club."

I chuckled. "Bi, remember. Same as you."

He laughed and watched me as the elevator doors opened. His eyes scanning my face. "Are you sure you know what you're doing?"

"I hope so."

Chapter 16

Brock

Sampson whined by the door. He was waiting for Declan to come home with as much anticipation as I was. But he seemed to know more than I did about when he'd arrive. It was like Sampson could detect when Declan was close.

He had texted me when he landed to let me know he was on his way back. I was sure after so long on the road he'd be exhausted. It wasn't easy traveling all the time. Just when he'd get settled here, he'd have to leave again. Some of the trips were short, others not so much, like the one he was just on.

I had a late lunch in the oven, keeping warm for him. I made comfort food since he'd been gone. I figured he could use some home cooking. I had macaroni and cheese I made from scratch, as well as grilled chicken and creamy mashed potatoes.

While I was pacing the floor, my eyes repeatedly drifting to Sampson where he sat by the door, I kept thinking about what it had been like with Declan gone. Lali came over a couple nights to keep me company. She had seen right through me, and I ended up spilling things to her about Declan. About how we kissed but hadn't gone further. I left out the fact that I jerked off so much I was surprised my dick wasn't sore. Then again, while Declan had been gone, my libido fled as well. It seemed like it was specifically attached to him while he was here on his days off or playing home games.

Now that he was almost here again, my body felt like a live wire, energy coursing through me, even though I didn't sleep well last night. While Declan was away, I made a decision. I was going to tell him I wanted to try this thing with him, not that I knew what it was. It wasn't like we were committing ourselves to a relationship. He wanted to have fun, while I wanted a little more. Not a full-on boyfriend type of thing but not only here for his pleasure either.

I needed a connection to him. He wasn't some nameless guy I hooked up with in a dark alcove of a club. He was Declan, the guy I'd been lusting after since he moved in with me. The guy I shouldn't want yet couldn't seem to stay away from.

Was that part of the allure to this? That I promised I wouldn't touch Declan. Was it driving me to want to do just that, in some sort of rebellious thing against being told what to do? I agreed to it. I realized now I shouldn't have. But I couldn't go back. I had to work with what I had going forward. That didn't mean the guilt wasn't still there; however, it took a back seat to the way I felt for Declan.

Scrubbing my hands over my face, I paused in my pacing and groaned. Who knew my relaxing retirement was going to be more stressful than it was when I was playing for the Sandpipers?

All of the sudden, Sampson stood and pressed his nose to where the door met the frame. Then I heard the garage door open. The dog was good. He knew Declan was here before any sounds were made.

I dropped down on the couch and tried to look relaxed with a book in my hand. It took me a moment to realize I was holding it upside down. That wouldn't look suspicious at all.

Sampson began his happy dance with his curved tail wagging and little whines as I heard Declan climbing the stairs. The door opened and I glanced up over the top of my book to see the man I'd missed while he was gone.

Declan came through the doorway, pushed it shut behind him, dropped his bags, then went to his knees on the floor to greet Sampson. I wish he got on his knees for me, too. Maybe he would if he still wanted this thing between us.

I wasn't someone who wanted to dominate another. I'd go to my knees for him, too, though I was sure my body would protest about it. But with the thought of seeing him down there for me... I was getting hard, reminding me it was a good idea I put on shorts with an actual button and zipper rather than the basketball ones I preferred to wear. I also had on a longer T-shirt to hide the bulge I was sure I was sporting now. No need to show all my cards right away.

Placing the book down, it was time for me to greet Declan as well and try to pretend I wasn't sitting around waiting for him to come back. Waiting for this moment when I could lay my eyes on him again. See those dimples when he smiled at me.

By the time I made my way over to the door, Declan was standing after getting lots of love from Sampson. The dog was thrilled to have him here. I knew whenever Declan moved out to a new place, I wouldn't be the only one who would be sad to see him go.

Declan's eyes held mine. How did he get more handsome while he was gone? "Hey, Brock."

Need surged through me. Not the kind to throw him down on the closest surface and ravage his mouth and body, but the kind that needed to touch him. Needed to feel him. Reaching forward, I pulled him into my arms. He let out a startled gasp but then brought his arms around me. Given our similar heights, his smooth cheek rested against mine which I hadn't shaved since he left, letting my beard grow in.

"I'm glad you're back," I told him quietly, suddenly unable to talk at a higher volume.

Declan hummed low in his throat, then tucked his face near my neck and inhaled. I wondered what he thought about being this close to me. Did he like the scents of my body wash and shampoo? The light amount of cologne I put on knowing he'd be back today?

I didn't realize having him in my arms would feel so good, so right. I was reluctant to release him, but my dick was trying to make its way out of my shorts, and I didn't need Declan aware of just how much I wanted him. Though I shouldn't have worried because when we separated, he took a moment to adjust himself.

He smiled, not embarrassed by his reaction to me. "Not that I'm complaining about the new affection, but did something change while I was gone?"

I blushed, which was absurd. I was a big, burly guy. I was a retired NFL player. Yet, Declan made me nervous. "I did a lot of thinking while you were on the road. Let's eat and we can talk." At least if I was eating, I'd be able to pause and focus on something else as I gathered my thoughts and said what I wanted to.

"Do I have time for a shower?"

"Of course. I'll get everything ready."

Declan grabbed his things and went upstairs. I didn't inhale a deep breath until I heard his door shut. Butterflies were flying in my stomach, causing my nerves to ratchet higher. I never thought I'd have that feeling when it came to another person, yet here I was.

Shutting off the oven, I took the food out in the covered dishes then plated everything and took it over to the table. It was a lot for a late lunch, but I was okay with that. I had to do something to keep myself occupied earlier.

Only a short time passed before Declan was coming back downstairs and striding to the table. "This looks great. You didn't have to go to all this trouble." I quirked an eyebrow at him. He knew how much I liked to cook. He chuckled. "I wasn't used to this kind of cooking while I was gone."

"I'm sure you had great meals between room service and restaurants."

"It was good but after a while, it got old. I craved home-cooked meals like this." He took a seat opposite me at the table.

We both dug in, Declan a little more enthused than me. After a few bites, he put down his fork and looked at me expectantly. I guess it was my turn to talk. I needed to explain why I wrapped him in my arms when he came through the door.

"While you were gone..." I cleared my throat, took a drink, and made myself focus on Declan instead of my plate. "I thought a lot about things."

"Which things?" His smile bordered on a smirk. He wanted me to say it, spell it out.

"The kiss. How I feel. Where we go from here."

"Tell me how you feel, Brock."

"I..." I scratched the back of my neck. The butterflies needed to calm down. "I want more."

"How much more?"

My face heated. "God dammit, you're going to make me say it, aren't you?" I grumbled. I wasn't angry and there was none of it in my tone.

Declan's smile was still firmly in place. "I need to hear it."

"I want to kiss you again. I want to touch you, you to touch me. I want to get to know you intimately, but we need to set some ground rules."

"Sure, a relationship with rules, makes sense."

I glared at him. "I didn't say it was a relationship."

Holding up his hands, he said, "My bad. Go on."

"I haven't been with a guy in public before, Dec. I've never gone on a date with one, kissed one while out, done anything that would imply to the outside world that I'm gay. My parents don't even know. So, if you and me are going to do..." I waved my hand between us, "something, then we have to go at my pace. I'm not ready to be out in public with a guy. I don't know what this is between us, if anything, but I would like to test the waters."

"Test the waters? I'm not sure whether to be flattered or skeptical."

I growled, "Are you trying to make this difficult for me? I don't want to be out there with someone who only wants a fling. If I'm going to tell the world I'm gay, I'd rather do it with a partner by my side. But you and me... You want fun." Declan could be that partner. I wasn't going to tell him I wanted him to be. It was too much pressure.

I had to put some rules in place. I wanted to ease into this. People probably wouldn't care about me since I was a retired player, but being seen on Declan's arm, the media would latch on to it, given how much they loved the Emperors here. There was also the fact that Ethan couldn't know. My guilt reared its ugly head again.

Instead of responding right away, Declan pushed his chair back and stood.

"Are you done eating? I thought you'd like this meal." Maybe I left it to warm too long and it started to dry out.

He rounded the table until he was standing before me, causing me to tip my head back to look up at him. The next thing I knew, Declan straddled my lap. My hands immediately went to his waist. I'd never had a man on me like this. My only encounters were quick to get off and leave. No sense of intimacy.

"Brock," he said my name gently. My eyes went to his. "I'm only teasing, not trying to make your life hard." He squirmed a little on my lap. "Though, if another part of you was hard, I would know exactly how to handle it." I dropped my head to his chest and groaned. He laughed and it vibrated through to me. "I promise to take it slow. I won't do anything you don't want to. And we don't have to declare to the world we're fucking."

Leaning back, I asked, "Fucking?"

He brushed his lips along my cheek until his breath skated over my ear. "If that's what you want."

I shivered, my dick strained against my fly. "Dec, please." How did I go from irritated to lust drunk so fast? Oh, wait. It was the gorgeous man on my lap, whispering to me while his hand skated down my chest to my waist.

"Tell me what you need, Brock. I've been away for over a week, thinking of nothing but playing ball and you."

My fingers dug into his hips and with every ounce of willpower I had, I pushed him gently from my lap, knowing if I didn't, I'd let him do anything he wanted to me. And I wanted that so much, but Declan wasn't a random guy in a club. He was so much more. I needed to slow us down. "Food," I rasped out.

His laugh filled the space between us causing me to smile. "Okay, let's eat. No reason to let this food go to waste." With a wink, he moved back to his side of the table.

It was my turn to adjust my dick before I picked up my fork and forced myself to focus on my plate again.

My pace. He told me I could set it. If only he knew I wanted to throw my pace out the window and explore every inch of his body with my tongue.

While a part of me felt like a weight had been lifted and those butterflies turned from making my stomach feel nervous to pure joy, I had to learn to walk before I ran. I couldn't just have a fling with Declan. Without having any previous relationships, I wanted to do things with him right, even if I wasn't sure if there was any kind of future for us, especially with that guilt from Ethan hanging over my head.

But touching Declan, having him so close to me, it didn't feel wrong. It felt perfect.

Chapter 17

Declan

The food was delicious, even if it was the furthest thing from my mind. Brock wanted to eat, so we did just that. The only thing I could focus on was the way his hard dick pressed into me when I sat on his lap. I watched his Adam's apple bob when he swallowed each bite. It was absolute torture sitting across from Brock and not touching him. But the best kind of torture would be made all the sweeter when I could finally get my hands on him.

Walking through the door, I honestly never expected Brock to pull me into a hug or tell me he wanted more. It had thrown me off enough that I went right to teasing Brock to hide my own feelings. Since I was a kid, I'd use teasing as a way to deflect attention away from myself. I didn't want Brock to know what I really wanted between the two of us. Actually, I didn't think he was ready to know that, so I pushed it down and put a smile on my face.

Although, I had to admit his reaction to the word 'relationship' hurt. I wanted it more than anything. I would just have to convince Brock I was worth it. That *we* could be worth it. For now, I'd take things at his pace, all while showing him exactly how much he meant to me. How much more we could be together.

I continued to watch Brock, and I knew if we were ever going to get through our meal without me attacking him over the table, I needed something to focus on while we ate.

"What did you do while I was on the road?" It felt like such a ridiculous question since I now knew his routine inside and out. Only, it was the safest thing to talk about since everything else would not have me moving slowly with him.

Brock scratched the back of his neck, which I'd learned was a sign of his nerves. "I, umm, I actually came out to my brother."

I stopped with the fork midway to my mouth. "You did?"

Brock nodded. "After our conversation about Ethan, I realized it was time to come clean to him. He deserved to know."

"Feels like a weight off your shoulders?"

Brock blew out a breath. "You have no idea. Each person I tell is like I'm keeping less and less of myself from the world."

Even though I told myself this conversation was to keep me from thinking about Brock's hands and lips on my body, it didn't stop me from reaching across the table and laying my hand over his. "I'm glad."

We sat there for a minute. The connection not about sex or desire but about comfort and caring. Exactly what I expected it could be from a relationship with Brock. When I brought my hand back to pick up my fork, a comfortable silence fell over the table as we ate. Brock finished first and leaned back in his chair, watching me with a smile on his face.

"I thought about something else while you were gone."

I finished my plate and set down my fork. "And what was that?"

"Going back to college to further my education. I went online and started the application process."

"Congratulations. When will you hear from the school?" I picked up my bottle of water and took a sip.

"I haven't submitted it yet. As an alumnus, the application is only formal paperwork. Espen University turns away very few of their former students when they're seeking advanced degrees."

"So you'd start in the fall?"

"Maybe. Then you can make me dinner." Brock laughed.

"I don't know that we really want to go there unless you enjoy food poisoning with your homework," I joked, but my mind was reeling.

September was three months away. Did Brock really expect me to still be living here by then? I wouldn't lie to myself and admit that wasn't exactly what I wanted. I hadn't even bothered to look at any places to rent or buy.

To hear him say it though made butterflies take off in my stomach.

We talked a little more about his college program and what that would look like for him. Apparently, Brock had been thinking about it for all the years he'd been playing professional sports, which surprised me.

"Have you thought what you want to do after baseball?" he asked.

"Honestly? No." I finished off the bottle of water and replaced the cap. "Baseball has been my dream since I was a little kid. I got my degree in finance, but it was never something I really wanted to do. I knew it would pay well if I couldn't make it to the majors."

Brock scoffed. "Like that was ever going to happen."

"Hey, you never know. I was one of the lucky ones. I look at the guys down in the minors who may never have their shot and work for peanuts compared to what I make."

"You were always going to make it. I just knew it."

I smiled. "Thanks. I guess when I get close to retirement, I'll start thinking about what's next. With the travel and, hopefully, another ten or twelve years in the game, I may be ready to sit on my ass all day and do nothing."

Brock laughed, the sound warm and rich as it settled over me. "Speaking of doing something, what did you want to do for the rest of the day? You don't have a game until tomorrow night, right? Do you want to go down to the beach for a while?"

"Actually, I'd love to put my feet up and binge watch some TV. I've been *on* for days. For tonight, I want to be myself and just bum around the house. Is that okay with you?" And maybe I was hoping that might include more kissing. Kissing Brock was the most electrifying feeling in the world.

I picked up my plate and carried it to the kitchen, placing it in the dishwasher. With the remnants of lunch put away, I wandered around the couch and dropped down onto the soft cushions. One thing no one told you about playing professional baseball—the sheer exhaustion after a long stretch on the road. Hopping from hotel to game to a new hotel a few nights later. It was draining. I'd been serious when I told Brock I missed the homemade meals. Missed the atmosphere that came with them. Five-star restaurants could never compare to something cooked at home.

Brock took the seat next to me. I grabbed the remote and flipped through the channels, looking for something that would catch both of our attention. Or maybe, better yet, I needed something that wouldn't catch either of our attention and we could find something else to do.

The whole situation seemed awfully familiar, except this time I knew what Brock was thinking, at least some of it. He wanted to kiss me. I could see it in his eyes while we ate. Not that I planned on doing a damn thing about it besides being here whenever he was ready. I promised we'd go at his pace, which meant he needed to make the first move.

I settled on a reality show about crabbing in Alaska, my attention completely focused on the man beside me. It felt like electric currents were zapping back and forth between us with the tension filling the room.

Brock sat on the couch, each muscle completely rigid. I worried one small little poke might break him.

He was nervous about this entire thing, and for that, I couldn't blame him. I'd been out in public with men and women. There were also times I was out with friends, nothing more. No one ever speculated about Ayden and me when we had dinner together.

I moved closer to Brock until our shoulders were touching. I turned my head to look at him and found him already staring at me.

"I wasn't kidding when I said we would take this at your pace. I won't push you for anything more than you're ready for. If we want to be out in public together, we can be friends. No one has to know what happens behind these doors and walls besides us."

He didn't say a word. Instead, I watched as he lifted his hand to cup my face. I didn't look away. Heat burned in his eyes. The desire to have so much more, yet there just below that was a bit of fear. Maybe fear of the unknown. Fear of something new.

I didn't know, nor did I care, as he moved his mouth to mine and I got my second taste of Brock Richmond.

And let me tell you, it was way fucking better than the first.

This time, I knew where it would lead. To Brock's bed tonight? No. I had a feeling we would make it there someday, though. That made my second taste fantastic because I knew it wouldn't be the last. I still savored every second of his lips on mine.

The way his body trembled when his tongue slid across the seam of my lips, begging for entrance. Unlike earlier, when I was more than happy to tease Brock, I wouldn't torture myself by denying him anything. I parted my lips and let his tongue tangle with mine. Slowly, we moved until we faced one another.

I pulled my leg up onto the sofa so I could get even closer. My hands ran down his chest to the hem of his shirt and I teased the fabric, giving Brock a chance to stop me. When he didn't, I slipped my hands beneath it and got my first touch of his chest. Course hair met my fingertips and my dick jerked. There was nothing as sexy on this earth as a man with dark, wiry hair on his chest. Unlike my own smooth skin, I found Brock's furry pecs to be such a fucking turn-on.

If I didn't think it would freak him out, I'd yank his shirt off over his head and push him down onto the couch so I could run my tongue over every inch of him.

I kept up the exploration of his chest until I found his nipples, the little tight buds begging for attention. I pinched one between my fingers and rolled it around. Brock yanked his lips away from me and watched as I continued to caress and tug on his nipples.

Brock flattened my hand against his chest. When I glanced up into his face, harsh, panting breaths left him. His dick strained against his zipper. The T-shirt I pushed up no longer hiding the evidence of his arousal. He looked lower and that light pink flush was back. Brock reached down and adjusted himself.

"I don't think I'm ready for what comes next if you keep touching me."

My own cock throbbed, and I knew I needed to jerk off in the shower before going to bed. For now, I'd simply enjoy Brock's company since this was all way more than just sex. I pulled my hands from out below his and faced forward, adjusting myself. No way would I let Brock too far from me. I made sure our thighs were touching at every point possible.

Brock's breathing slowed, along with mine. He rested his arm along the back of the couch. I took immediate advantage and cuddled into his side. He froze and I thought for a split second he might get up and move. Then, he wrapped his arm around my shoulder and held me tighter to him.

Snuggled into his warmth, the exhaustion from the lack of sleep and worry hit me. The last thing I remembered was Brock's arm around me and the storm headed for the boat on TV.

Hopefully, there were no storms between the two of us.

Chapter 18

Brock

A week had gone by with Declan playing two home series during that time. It was nice having him here. Too bad he was leaving again tomorrow. This time he was heading south to Georgia and Florida.

There had been a lot more kissing between us. And even some quick hand jobs. I wanted to kick myself for deciding to go slow. Every time he touched me, I wanted to rip his clothes off and sink into him. Or have him inside me. I didn't even care which one it was. I just wanted him.

I was smiling as I sat on the deck facing the ocean. Sampson was by my side. The sky was darkening, looking like a summer storm was blowing in. I loved them, especially when I got to watch as they rolled through.

Footsteps on the stairs leading up to my deck caused me to turn. Declan was inside packing, so I knew it wasn't him. Turning, I found Reed with his light blond hair wet, hanging loosely to his shoulders. He was shirtless with small droplets of water still clinging to his skin. A blue striped towel was in one hand.

It wasn't uncommon for Reed to just pop over if he saw me on the deck. If I had been paying any bit of attention to the path, I would have seen him walk up.

He dropped down into the chair next to mine. Sampson was right there begging for attention. Reed pushed his wet hair back then petted Sampson's head, causing the short fur there to spike up a little.

"I can feel the electricity in the air," Reed said, tipping his head back against the chair to look at the sky. "I didn't want to get caught out there when it hit."

"Smart move." The ocean was not the place to be when it was thundering and lightning.

"Anything new?"

"Not really." I wasn't about to blurt out the fact that Declan and I were fooling around. That was no one's business but ours. Though Lali knew. That was what happened when she popped in Thursday afternoon to drop off a book she thought I'd like. She got a front-row seat to me nuzzling Declan's neck, while my hands gripped his ass as our clothed dicks rubbed together.

Lali wasn't a shy person, so it didn't faze her in the least. She laughed, gave Sampson some love quick, dropped the book on the counter, then left saying she didn't want to interrupt. I got a text later that night telling me she wouldn't be stopping by like that again unless she knew Declan was on the road. She didn't beg me for information or try to ask what Declan and I were to each other. That wasn't her. She knew when I was ready, I'd tell her.

"I'm starting a business," Reed said.

"Really? Doing what?" Reed had gone to college for two years, getting his associate's in business. He didn't like college, but his parents convinced him to hang in for two years then he could stop. And he did. Since then, from what he'd told me, he'd been floating from job to job, never finding his passion.

"I want to open a gym. A couple friends and I were talking and we're going to do it together. Each will own a third of the business. We each bring something different to it. Liam is a dietician and Nolan is a personal trainer. We've all been doing jobs for other people and decided to pool our money and do something for us." Reed still lived at home. I was sure he was saving money and his parents were probably going to help him get the business up and running as well. They had the money to afford it.

"Good for you. Let me know when you're ready and open, I'll come by." I didn't like working out in public gyms. It was one of the reasons I kept the equipment I needed in my house. But by the smile on Reed's face, I knew I said the right thing. Hopefully he didn't take what I said for more than it was.

"I definitely will."

Thunder cracked out in the distance. The storm was getting closer.

Everyone seemed to have their lives together but me. I started that application to go back to college but had been so wrapped up with thoughts of Declan that I hadn't submitted it yet. I needed to do it. Get the ball rolling. Granted, I could sit around this house for the rest of my life and not want for anything. I had enough money to live that way, but I'd go stir-crazy. I needed a purpose. Something to do.

Reed and I slipped into a comfortable silence. I was grateful he wasn't trying to hit on me. He was a nice guy but not the one I saw myself with. No, the man I wanted was in the house where I should be. I was going to miss him while he was gone. At least I had one task to do once he left. Maybe I needed to create to-do lists to keep myself busy.

The sliding door opened behind me. I didn't bother turning. Declan's scent drifted to me with a gust of the air-conditioned breeze that came with him. It was hot out here, humid. The impending storm would break it slightly but not enough.

"Hi, Declan," Reed said. I turned and caught Reed's smile. It wasn't the same flirtatious one he usually gave me. If he started to show interest in Declan, I knew I'd get jealous. Which was ridiculous. I didn't have any claim over the man. We weren't exclusive. We were barely more than friends.

I focused on the ocean again as it started becoming a little choppier. I wanted so much with Declan, and I was the only one standing in my way. No, that wasn't right. Ethan was standing in my way, too. I got a text from him earlier, checking in on me. He did that sometimes when he was asking about his brother. But I never had anything to report. He kept trying to get me out there to date. If he lived closer, I had a feeling he'd drag me out to a club.

The situation with Declan was everything I wanted and so screwed up at the same time. I hated hiding how I promised his brother I'd stay away from him. It was right up there with how I felt breaking that very promise.

Declan crouched down to pet Sampson. He smiled up at me and it turned me to mush inside. How did this man have that effect on me? One innocent smile and I wanted to launch myself at him.

"All packed?" I asked.

"Yeah. I'm not ready to leave again, though."

"I know, but you've been playing great."

"You have," Reed cut in. "You've been unstoppable since coming to Espen." He grinned. "I still can't believe one of the Emperors is living next door to me with one of the Sandpipers."

"Ex," I reminded him.

"Whatever. My point stands. I'm a lucky guy." Reed's gaze skated down my chest and up my bare arms. I had on a sleeveless shirt that fit loosely, leaving my arms on display. I didn't wear it on purpose to catch his attention. I didn't even know he'd be here. It was one of the most comfortable shirts I owned.

Another crack of thunder sounded, this time it was closer. Sampson stood.

"You better go now before it starts to rain," I told him and pointed to the stairs. For a moment I didn't think he was going to go, but then Reed stood saying he should get home as well. The two of them went down to the sand and Reed let himself out through the gate in the fence.

Raindrops started to fall as Sampson was coming back up faster than normal. He wasn't a fan of the rain.

The three of us went inside and I closed and locked the slider behind us. Depending on how long the storm lasted, Sampson might not go out again tonight.

The room was quiet, the lights off. Nothing but a few flashes of lightning to brighten the dim space every now and then. Declan stood in front of me, so close I could touch him, yet I kept my hands by my sides. I wanted him but wasn't sure how far I should go. One thing I knew for certain, I was past hand jobs.

"Brock." My name on his lips was like the lightning outside but instead of striking in the distance, it lit a fire in my veins.

I reached out and tugged him to me. My lips met his in a rough kiss. One that would bruise if I kept it going like it was. I eased back enough to lick along his lips. As soon as his were parted, I dove in like a starved man. I wasn't normally like this with Declan. I let him lead most of the time, but something inside me had come loose seeing him in here. Knowing he was about to leave for the road again.

Our bodies met from hips to lips and we started a slow grind against each other, but it wasn't nearly enough. "Upstairs," I said when I leaned back to take in some much-needed air.

Declan didn't need to hear the words twice. He took my hand in his and pulled me toward the stairs then up them, where he stopped in the hallway. My room had a king-sized bed where his was a queen, so I tugged him toward mine then pushed the door shut behind us. I didn't want Sampson to interrupt us.

Standing before me, Declan waited for me to make the next move. He was so good about letting me lead the way.

"I want my mouth on you," I whispered as I reached for his shorts. He had on basketball ones like me, so they were easy to push down along with his boxer briefs.

"Anything," came his reply.

Instead of dropping to my knees in front of him and regretting how the years playing football battered my body, I nudged him toward the bed. He kicked off his shorts then lifted his shirt over his head. I did the same, needing more contact with him tonight. Declan climbed onto the bed and settled on his back in the middle of it. I wasted no time moving between his legs as he spread them wider.

I gave him one last look. The room was dark. I was only able to make out that his eyes were on me and his lips were parted. Leaning down, I licked a strip up his dick. It jumped beneath my tongue. When I got to the tip, I tongued the slit to gather the precum there to take into my mouth. He was salty and slightly bitter. Delicious.

Taking hold of his base, I held his dick up so I could engulf him in my mouth. His hips punched upward, but thanks to my grip on him, he didn't gag me as he went. With my free hand, I started playing with his balls, gauging his reaction to everything I did.

"Fuck, Brock." I loved the way his voice sounded wrecked. I did that to him. It gave me a boost of confidence. I wasn't overly experienced with blow jobs. I'd given some over the years, but I wasn't anywhere near the point where I could deep throat him.

Declan's fingers wove into my hair to hold me still as he began to thrust into my mouth at the pace that felt best for him. I was hard as steel in my shorts. More precum hit my tongue. Declan's body was coiled tight.

The storm was so close, thunder rattled the windows as rain pelted them. Lightning struck so bright I was able to catch of glimpse of Declan's blown pupils.

Reaching down, I slipped my hand down to my dick out. I couldn't take it anymore. I needed to come as badly as he did. With the sounds he was making, the way his body was moving, it was making me hotter for him.

"You feel so good," he moaned. "So fucking perfect."

I kept at him, not slowing down, even when he told me he was close to coming. I wanted him to let go in my mouth. I wanted to take more of him into me. Just the thought had my orgasm rising to the surface as my hand flew over my dick.

"Coming!" he called out a moment before the first drop of his cum hit my tongue.

That triggered my own climax. I moaned around his length as I painted his leg with my release. My body shook with the force of what was happening while I drank down everything Declan could give me.

I finally gave in and let him pull my head off him. I rested my forehead against his thigh while I caught my breath. Tears had built in my eyes from him using me in the best way. I had no doubt if he had pushed down my throat, those tears would have been streaming down my cheeks.

"Holy shit," he said in between gasps of air.

"I know." My voice was hoarse.

Declan tugged on my hair gently. "Come up here."

"In a second." I stood from the bed and went into the en suite to wet a cloth so I could clean his leg off. Back in the bathroom, I threw it in the hamper and washed my hands.

The storm was drifting into the distance when I climbed onto the bed, settling on my side next to Declan. He rolled over to face me. then leaned forward to press his lips to mine.

"Is this the kind of sendoff I can expect every time I leave for the road?" he teased.

"Possibly. Just imagine what you're coming home will be like."

For the first time in so long, I felt amazing. I was able to be myself and let go. Be someone I never allowed myself to be before. Declan saw every part of me. No disguises were needed. It was freeing.

Chapter 19

Declan

Dirt and sweat swirled down the drain. Another long game and a win. Couldn't really complain much when the innings were long with the Emperors bringing in the runs. The atmosphere in the locker room was electric. There was still a long way to the World Series, but things were looking good for a run at the title—a first for me.

Yet, the excitement wasn't there, not yet. A little of it had to do with the fact that a season could change at any moment. One minute, your team is up playing the best baseball of their lives, then, the next, not a single player on your team can connect with the ball.

More than that were the dreams about Brock's lips as they slid up and down my cock. It kept me from focusing on anything else when I wasn't on the field. Brock's warm mouth had me coming in record time, something I definitely wanted to experience again. Not that it was happening anytime soon. We still had one more game in this series and another in Florida before we could head back home to Espen.

My cock ached. If it weren't for my teammates in the shower stalls around me, I might have given in and taken it in my hand, if only to take the edge off. Instead, I gritted my teeth and finished my shower. There would be plenty of time for that back in my room, with the shower all to myself, and of course my left hand to keep me company.

I walked out of the showers toward my temporary locker. While many stadiums had a decent-sized clubhouse for the visiting team, we happened to be in the oldest stadium in the pros, and their visitors' clubhouse hadn't been renovated since long before I was born. Crammed into the room, I knew none of my teammates would be hanging around here long. After a shower, just enough to get clean, they'd throw on clothes and take the shuttle back to the hotel where they could spread out and relax. Maybe a few of them would go out, but I wasn't in the mood.

Dressed and more than ready to get out of here, I navigated through the space, dodging moving bodies as I went. I waved to the guys who called out my name, breathing a sigh of relief when I stepped into the hall. Even when I played with the Backfins, this was my least favorite stadium to play in.

"Declan, hold up." I glanced over my shoulder to see Vander jogging down the hall toward me. I waited for him to catch up. "You ran out of there fast."

"That place is way too tight for me. They need a good remodel."

He chuckled. "They do. Supposedly, the plans are there, but they wanted to get the main clubhouse done first."

"I can't really blame them for that." I hiked my bag higher onto my shoulder as we stepped out into the sticky night air. "You don't seem to be in a hurry to stay?"

A smirk lifted the corner of his mouth. "Nope. Promised Evan I'd video chat with him tonight when I got back to the hotel."

There was no way that Evan and Vander were just talking. I hadn't met Evan yet, but from the stories I heard, Vander and Evan liked to fuck like bunnies, and they weren't the least bit shy about where they were when they did it. Thank fuck, I didn't have the room next to his. Whoever it was probably wouldn't be getting any sleep until the early hours of the morning.

We climbed onto the shuttle and the cool breeze of the air conditioner hit me in the face. "Fuck, could it be any more humid?"

Vander chuckled. "Probably, but if you aren't used to it, it can be a bitch. Ayden says you grew up in Pennsylvania?"

"Yeah. Summers were hot and humid but nothing like this. I always forget how bad it is until we have to travel south for the summer. What about you?"

"I grew up in South Florida, I'm used to this shit." Vander flopped down onto one of the seats. "Doesn't mean I don't enjoy the cool blast of an air conditioner."

Laughing, I took the seat in the row across from him. With no one else on the shuttle, there was no reason to squish in. Two shuttles would run back and forth between the stadium for the next hour or so, giving the players a chance to go back to the hotel when they were ready. Vander tugged his phone from his bag, his fingers flying over the screen, no doubt telling Evan he was on his way back. The love in his eyes for the man was evident.

The smile on his face made me miss Brock even more. Problem was, I couldn't talk with anyone about it. Coming out was up to Brock. Until then, I had to figure out a way to get through the next week without missing him too much. Then, it hit me. I should take a page out of Vander's playbook. Why couldn't I video chat with Brock? It would be a way to see each other and not be so lonely with my left hand.

I took my phone from my pocket and texted Brock. No way would he be asleep yet. If there was one thing I learned, it was that he stayed up and watched my games no matter where we were playing.

Me: Almost back to the hotel. Get your laptop out.

Brock: My laptop? Why?

His replies were always quick after a game.

Me: Because I want to see you. And I can't do that good enough through the phone.

Brock: You want to video chat?

I chuckled and saw Vander turn his head in my direction for a second before going back to his phone.

Me: Yes. So be ready in fifteen minutes.

We pulled into the front horseshoe of the hotel, and I followed Vander down the steps and through the doors into the lobby. Silently, Vander and I stepped onto the elevator to head up to our rooms. Excitement burned through me. I'd never done anything like this before. I wasn't the least bit shy, but I'd always been happy to settle for someone on the road when I was feeling restless. Never had I been with only one person where it was more than just sex.

Vander was still typing away on his phone when the doors opened and he stepped out onto his floor.

"Enjoy your night."

Vander turned right before the doors shut. "Don't worry, I will."

I laughed at the lust written all over his face as the doors closed. Although, I had a feeling I'd see the same on my face if I looked in the mirror. I wanted Brock and I wanted him badly. If I couldn't have him in person, then I was going to watch him fall apart in front of me.

Now the problem would be getting Brock to participate. He was pretty shy, all things considered, which might require a little push of my own. I unlocked the door to my room and dropped my stuff right by it. The suite had a large living room, much larger than I was used to. Seemed my agent was able to negotiate a bigger room with my trade. I hadn't cared about it before, but tonight I was more than happy to have the privacy.

A relaxing shower could wait until after I got rid of the pent-up sexual tension of the last few days. I went right for my bag to grab my tablet. No need for my small-ass phone screen. I wanted to see everything.

Once I had it set up on the table in front of the couch, where I could have a good view of him and he would see me, I stripped out of my clothes and sat down on the couch. I hit dial and waited.

"Hey—" The picture connected and Brock came into view. "Why are you naked?" He swallowed hard.

I reached down and took my shaft in my hands, loving the way Brock's eyes followed the movement and his breathing picked up slightly.

"I wanted to see you and you to see me. All of me."

With an obvious effort, Brock lifted his gaze to mine. "I can definitely see... everything."

"I want to see you, too. Take off your clothes, Brock."

His eyes heated as a light pink hit his cheeks. He shook his head emphatically. "I can't do that."

"Yes, you can." I moved my hand up my now hard cock and didn't hide the moan that escaped my lips. I knew Brock would need more than that. "I've been so lonely these last few days, getting off in the shower by myself." I continued stroking, only stopping to rub my thumb over the tip, spreading the precum over my shaft. "I want to watch you come with me."

Brock reached down to adjust himself. "Dec," he whispered.

"That's a good start. Now slide your hand into your waistband."

"I... I've never... I'm not sure I can," he argued, even as his hand traveled toward the top of his gym shorts. The loose fabric did nothing to hide how hard he was. I knew he wanted this as badly as I did, he was just afraid to take the leap.

"You can. Now reach inside and pull out that beautiful dick so I can see it."

Mesmerized, his gaze riveted on me, Brock dipped his hand inside and slowly started to stroke himself. I kept stroking my own dick, loving the way Brock's pupils were blown wide. I knew he was past the point of fighting me, running on instinct alone. Time to keep pushing.

"Shove your pants down. I want to see that gorgeous cock as it leaks all over your hand." A feral groan tore from Brock as he lifted his hips and shoved his shorts down his thighs. "That's it. Look at that dark purple head straining to get to me."

Brock moaned. His eyes started to fall closed.

"Nope, keep them open, baby. I need you to watch me." Brock opened his eyes again. I could barely tell where the dark brown irises began. "Now, the shirt. Wouldn't want you to come all over it."

Brock yanked the shirt over his head. "You're so sexy. I'll never have the tight abs you do."

"You don't need them. You're perfect in every way to me."

Brock's hand flew faster over his cock. "I'm so close."

I knew the feeling. The taboo feeling of watching each other when there were strangers right on the other side of the wall had me close to the edge, faster than I'd ever gotten there. A lot of that also had to do with the man on the other side of the call. This was perfect for the moment, but I wanted more, and it was time Brock knew how much I wanted him.

"Soon enough, I'm going to be home and I'll bury myself deep inside that tight ass of yours or I'll get on all fours as you pound deep inside me."

"Declan!" Brock roared, his release painting his chest.

The way his eyes rolled in the back of his head and the sound of my name on his lips made it impossible to hold out any longer. The base of my spine tingled, and my vision blurred around the edges as I came on my chest.

Harsh breaths filled the space. When I finally was able to open my eyes again, I was glad to see that Brock hadn't tried to cover up, even as the orgasmic bliss faded. I knew he worried about the way he looked, but he had to be the sexiest man I'd ever seen.

"I miss you."

Brock smiled and everything was right in my world.

Chapter 20

Brock

My life had changed so much since Declan moved in with me. He was kind, generous, the single sexiest man I knew. But he brought out this whole other side of me. The one I had locked away and wasn't sure I'd ever be able to feel comfortable enough to let out. No, I wasn't fully out there, declaring to the world I was gay, but in the safety of my home, I was wholly myself.

I was so tired of staying home, though. I needed to get out of here and do something fun. Wasn't that what retirement was supposed to be like? I wasn't in my seventies, settling in for the rest of my life. I should be living, doing more than I was. And there was no one I wanted to do it with more than Declan.

He'd been patient with me, going at my pace. Not once had he complained about being cooped up in the house when he wasn't on the road. Maybe that was why. He was traveling a lot. Being here meant he could relax.

Today was the Fourth of July and I had plans for us. But I had to wait for Declan to get home first. I texted him last night, after they lost the series down in Florida, and asked if he'd be up for doing something today. I wanted to cheer him up. He immediately took it as the sexy kind of fun, but I quickly told him I wanted to go out. To consider it a date but not a date if that made any sense. I still had the horrible guilt with Ethan hanging over my head like a dark cloud. But I wanted Declan and me to do something outside of the house for once.

While Declan had been gone, I wrestled with myself about what to do regarding him. I talked at length about it with Lali. While she understood my problem, she said I was making more out of it than it needed to be. But she didn't know Ethan like I did. She didn't understand the depth of my relationship with him—with his whole family—and how that factored into what I was doing with Declan. It wasn't just the two of us in this. It was both families. I didn't want anything to come between all of us.

What I needed to do was grow a set of balls and talk to Ethan. Only, every time the thought entered my mind, I broke out in a sweat and my heart started racing. I wasn't someone who suffered with a lot of anxiety. Although, this thing with Declan had my head spinning. There was nothing bad about us. Would Ethan see it that way? I didn't think so. He'd be angry at me for breaking the promise I made him. The one thing he'd asked me not to do.

The door opening caused me to break away from my thoughts. Putting my inner turmoil aside, I stood from where I was sitting on the couch and went to greet Declan. Of course, Sampson got there first.

After saying hi to the good boy, Declan stood and gave me that smile of his that made my stomach flutter. He didn't give me the chance to debate how to greet him; he stepped forward until his arms were around me and his lips were on mine. I moaned, helpless to do anything but surrender to his touch and taste. Declan was everything I wanted in a boyfriend, in a partner. But we weren't there yet, and I wasn't sure if we ever could be.

Pulling back, I cupped his cheeks and smiled. He had a little bit of stubble, which was rough against my palms. "Good trip?"

"Yeah, glad to be home." Every time he referred to my house as his home, it caused those butterflies in my stomach to take flight.

Leaning forward, I kissed him again, this time slow and sweet before resting my forehead on his. If we kept at it like this, we'd never leave. "Are you sure you want to do something with me?"

Declan beamed. "Are you kidding? I get to go out with the hottest guy I know, and watch other people be jealous they aren't with him? Hell, yeah, I'm sure."

"You have that completely backward, but I'll take the compliment." No one had ever showed me attention like Declan did. I'd also never given anyone the opportunity to do so.

"I was going to suggest paintball but it's too hot outside, so what do you say to laser tag? I'm hoping it will be quieter today, considering the holiday. More people will be on the beach or throwing parties, enjoying the great weather."

"Sounds good to me. Let me get changed into something more comfortable and we'll get going."

With another peck on the lips, he went upstairs with his bags. I walked over to the kitchen to make sure Sampson had enough water in his bowl and then made sure the doors were locked. The last thing I wanted was someone drunk stumbling up here from the beach, thinking this was their rental. I'd be sure to set the alarm as we left, too.

Declan emerged a short time later in a pair of black basketball shorts and a white T-shirt. It was almost exactly what I had on, except my shirt was a mossy green. It would be easy to move around in and breathable because I knew we were going to work up a sweat running through the place.

We jumped into my SUV and made the short drive there. Traffic sucked but with the holiday it was to be expected. If I wanted to have fun with Declan, I had to do it when he had an off day. We'd suffer through the bumper-to-bumper people from out of town to get there.

The parking lot wasn't as empty as I had hoped, but it was nowhere near as bad as it would have been had it been a rainy day. Once the clouds opened up, people visiting looked for somewhere indoors to spend their time.

There was a kid behind the counter who couldn't have been older than eighteen. The moment he saw Declan, his eyes widened but he didn't ask for an autograph. Instead, he stumbled his way through the normal steps for anyone who showed up to play.

Laughing drew my attention to our right. I knew it sounded familiar when Reed emerged with his friends.

"Brock!" he called and came over. "You guys about to play?"

"Yeah, just got here."

No one would think of us coming here as anything but a couple of friends enjoying the game. A part of me was grateful for that. It kept what we were doing quiet. The other part of me felt horrible. If this had been anyone but Declan, I'd consider holding their hand, putting my hand on the small of their back, doing something to let the outside world know this man was with me. And I did want to claim Declan as mine, but he wasn't, no matter how much I wished it so. We were just two guys who fooled around.

Even as the thought entered my mind, I knew it was wrong. We were more than that. More than just a couple friends getting off together. But what we were eluded me. We needed to talk.

Reed turned back to his friends. "What do you say to another game?" They were all covered in a sheen of sweat from playing who knew how many games already. They agreed and the next thing I knew, it was Declan and me against Reed, Liam, and Nolan.

Five minutes into the game, I was trying to crouch behind a low wall with Declan pressed to my side. "I feel old," I panted out.

"Speak for yourself. This is fantastic."

I groaned. Declan's younger age and better shape was apparent. I was like someone's tired dad trying to run around with their kids. I could hardly keep up.

Declan shot me a smile then leaned in for a quick kiss. He licked his lips as he pulled back. No one could see us where we were hiding, especially with how dark it was. "Sorry, couldn't resist."

He deserved more than I was giving him, so I reached for the back of his neck and drew him in for a deeper kiss. One where I swept my tongue into his mouth and tasted him thoroughly. Declan's eyes were clouded with lust when I pulled back.

"Snap out of it," I told him. "I need you to get back out there and defend me. I'm old and slow."

He chuckled. "You can't kiss me like that and expect me not to be affected. Besides, you're not old. Slow, yeah, you are."

I shoved his shoulder. "Real nice."

Declan laughed loudly then clamped his mouth shut after remembering we were supposed to be hiding. "Consider this your warm-up to later tonight."

"Tonight?"

"You mentioned something about my coming home being better than my departure."

His words heated my body as I remembered when I had my mouth on him the night before he left for the road. I grumbled under my breath, trying to will my dick to behave. Now wasn't the time.

Footsteps drew closer, reminding me we were supposed to be playing a game, not making out in a darkened corner. Without saying another word, Declan slipped back into the chaos as sounds of someone being tagged rang out behind me.

After taking a couple deep breaths, I jumped out of hiding only to come face-to-face with a grinning Reed. His gun was raised, trained on my chest, but he didn't pull the trigger. "I can't shoot you. I got Declan, though." He winked.

In another life, I would have been attracted to Reed. He was a good-looking guy and his personality was great, but he couldn't compare to Declan. No one could.

I raised my gun and fired at Reed. He gasped, shock evident on his face. "What the hell?"

"That was for shooting Dec." Then I started running through the maze that was the second floor. Reed was hot on my tail, not giving me much room as he shot at me.

"Dec! I'm under attack!" I yelled. I had no idea where he was.

"You're on your own!" I heard called from the far side of the room as Reed laughed behind me.

There was no escaping Reed, though. Eventually, I just stopped running, admitting defeat. We found the rest of our friends and played hard for the time remaining. Then we played another game. The first one we lost but the second we won. By the time we were walking out of there, we were sweaty and gross, but we were all smiling wide.

I shook Liam's and Nolan's hands, thanking them for a good game. I tried to shake Reed's but he pulled me in for a quick hug instead. He invited us over to his house tonight since they were headed back there. Reed's parents chose to spend the holiday inland with some friends of theirs. I thanked him for the offer, although I was way too worn out to be up all night with these guys.

Declan said goodbye as well and thanked them for the invite, but he was tired from being on the road and wanted a night in. He could have gone to hang out with them, though chose not to. He decided to spend the night with me. I smiled, unable to help it.

Back in my SUV, we made the slow drive back to the house with the air-conditioning pumping from the vents. It felt good on my heated skin.

"Do you want to stop and pick up something to eat?" he asked. "I doubt you feel like cooking now."

"I have steaks I'm going to put on the grill. I also went to the farm stand and bought corn on the cob and everything to make salads." There was seriously nothing better than a Jersey tomato. I didn't care what anyone said. They hadn't lived until they tasted a tomato grown locally in the Garden State.

"Laser tag and a home-cooked meal? You sure know how to treat a guy well." He chuckled.

He meant it as a joke, but I took it a different way. If Declan was mine, if we were out and I didn't care who knew we were together, I'd treat him like a king. Give him whatever he wanted. He deserved no less.

"Hey," he said softly, drawing my eyes briefly to his. "You okay?"

"Yeah." I didn't want to voice my thoughts. Instead, I asked, "Do you want to watch fireworks from the deck tonight? Or we could go down to the beach. They always have a barge not far from the shore where they light them off."

"The deck is perfect. I've had enough of other people for the day. I just want to spend time with you."

I didn't know how Declan felt about me, but he was coming to mean a lot to me. More than anyone ever had. This thing we were doing was turning into more. I wanted him with every fiber of my being and had a feeling the only one standing in the way of us was me.

Chapter 21

Declan

The fireworks were beautiful in the night sky. Even more beautiful was the man beside me. He might not realize just how attractive he was to me. I'd have to do my best to keep reminding him. Over my last four years in baseball, I'd seen my fair share of fireworks shows. They were all spectacular, but nothing lived up to sitting with someone I cared about while watching them.

If only he was enjoying the show as much as I was. Something had been on Brock's mind from the moment I got home. I could see it in his eyes. Whatever it was, I wanted it gone. Brock could trust me with anything. If there was a problem we needed to solve, we would. But that was only if he talked to me.

There were times when I felt like there was a wall between us. Not all the time, just times like this when I knew there was something on his mind and, instead of talking to me about it, he kept it bottled up.

We couldn't keep dancing around things, and I couldn't continue to ignore the barrier making it harder for us to really push this thing between us to the next level. I reached over to Brock's hand, where it rested on the arm of his chair. I entwined our fingers and waited, hoping he wouldn't pull away. There was no one else out here. His neighbor and his friends had walked down to the beach long before the fireworks actually started.

He tightened his fingers and I turned back to watch as the finale began. One explosion after another. The sounds loud in the night but welcome, watching the pinks, blues, and greens. As the final light faded, and before the neighbors could come back and question Brock's hand in mine, I stood and pulled Brock to his feet.

"Come on. Let's go inside. I want you to myself for the rest of the night."

Brock followed me into the house without a word. I'd come home from the Florida series miserable. We'd lost every game and I definitely didn't play my best. An error on an easy throw to second cost us the last game. Even in the shit mood I was in, Brock found a way to bring me out of it. Seeing him and greeting him at the door with a kiss was the start. He'd looked so unsure when I walked in. I just needed his arms around me. The laser tag helped burn through the last bit of tension riding me.

Now it was a different kind of tension. The kind that required my hands on Brock and his on me. Everything would be perfect if I couldn't see Brock holding himself back. It was my turn to help him release the tension. I led Brock over to the couch and sat down, bringing him down with me. He lifted a brow when I sat a little away from him.

"I thought you had something else in mind when you said you wanted me to yourself." He smiled.

A smirk lifted the corner of my lips and I watched as Brock used his fingers to trace the dimple on my cheek. "Oh, there are a lot of things I want to do with you, but I think we need to talk first."

"Talk?"

Sampson was curled up in the corner on his bed. I watched him for a moment, the easy rise and fall of his chest. The sight seemed so simple. The two of us alone in the living room, the dark sky beyond. It was all so domestic. Not two roommates living together, but partners in life. Except, I didn't know what Brock wanted from me and, if my gut was correct, he had the same concerns.

"Yeah." I sucked in a deep breath. This was everything I always wanted and, at the same time, this simple conversation could be the downfall of it all. "I want to know what this is between us. What are we doing? Because I'm worried I see it as more than you do."

Brock's eyes widened. "I..." He stopped and blew out a breath. I braced myself for what came next. His eyes dropped from mine and my stomach sank until he lifted his gaze once again. This time, it was laser focused on me. "I wondered the same thing. You're on the road and I'm here—"

I covered his lips with my fingers. "You encompass every one of my thoughts on the road. I've wanted this since I was a teen watching you play football. I want us to be together. An actual *us*. If you're not ready for that in public, I understand. Brock, please hear me when I say, I don't want anyone else but you."

I moved my hand to let him speak. He opened and closed his mouth a few times before he was able to get the words out. "You wanted me when you were younger?" I nodded. "I can't... I didn't know. I want you, Dec. I want so much with you." He took my hand in his. "I was worried you didn't feel the same."

"Of course I want that with you." I slid closer and cupped his face with my other hand. "I've always wanted it."

He shook his head. "I'm nothing like the others you've been with. I'm older and my body isn't like yours. You're amazing out there on the field, while I sit here retired, applying for college again."

Straddling his lap, I thrust my hips forward, letting my hard dick slide against his. I bent down and bit on the lobe of his ear, then licked up the edge until he could hear me whisper, "This is how sexy I find you. Please don't ever doubt that again."

Brock cupped my ass, holding our groins tight together. "You feel so good. I can't resist you."

"Then, take me upstairs and I'll give you whatever you want." I captured Brock's lips with mine, not holding back. I wanted him to feel every ounce of my desire for him. Our tongues tangled, both of us fighting for dominance. My favorite thing about being with a guy—not having to be gentle. I loved it even more when the man in my arms was rough with me.

Brock sank his fingers into my hair and tugged my head back, breaking the connection of our lips. "Enough.

Get upstairs. I refuse to have you on the couch when there is much more space on my bed."

I scrambled off Brock's lap so fast Sampson lifted his head to see what was happening. Brock shook his head at the dog. "You stay right there." Sampson lowered his head again.

We raced up the stairs. It seemed we were both eager to have each other. Whatever way Brock wanted me, I was happy to give myself to him. He shut his bedroom door behind us and turned to face me. The heat that had been written on his face before was tamed by a bit of nerves. He stepped forward and took both of my hands in his.

"I've never done this before."

My eyes practically fell out of my head. "You've never had sex before?"

Brock rolled his eyes. "You know that's not true. If you'd let me finish."

I chuckled, loving the way this moment wasn't all lust and hormones. The best parts of our relationship were still there in the bedroom. Of course, I wanted to rip Brock's clothes off, but I also wanted what made things special between us. "Sorry. Go on."

He swallowed. "I've never bottomed before. Never trusted anyone to have me that way." He ran his thumb along my bottom lip. "It's different with you. I trust you."

A little more pressure than I expected tonight. It wasn't going to stop me from having Brock in a way no one else had. "I'll make it good for you."

"I know you will." Brock captured my lips. Not normally the aggressor, I loved the way he backed me up until my body slammed into the door.

Deep rumbling moans escaped me as I reached for the waistband of his shorts, shoving them to the floor with his boxer briefs. Brock's mouth attacked mine. His lips and tongue making it hard to think. To breathe. He moved back to take a breath and I took advantage, tugging off his shirt and tossing it to the floor.

"That's much better. Now, I just need to see you sprawled across the bed."

"That, I can do. You're still a little overdressed."

"A problem I plan to fix right now." I stripped out of my clothes in seconds. My rock-hard cock standing straight up, begging for the man in front of me.

Brock walked backward, stroking his dick. He was long and slightly curved. Just the thought of him sliding deep into my channel made my own dick leak. Tonight wasn't about that, though. Tonight, I was going to make Brock come like he never had before.

He sat down on the bed, never taking his eyes from mine, and slid up into the middle. "I can't wait to feel you inside me." Brock's hips punched up off the bed and he tightened his grip around his cock. "Touch me, Dec."

"Lube and condoms?" There was no way I was getting anywhere near Brock's dick without the supplies I needed. Once I had my hands on him, there would be no turning back.

"Top drawer." He pointed to the dresser next to me.

I turned and opened the drawer. Next to his boxers and socks I found an unopened box of condoms and a tube of lube. I tore open the box and grabbed one out.

With condom and lube in hand, I walked over to the bed and dropped the supplies I needed next to Brock.

His breathing sped as I climbed up from the bottom of the bed, running my hand along the inside of his leg. My fingers skimmed along his thigh; the course hairs rough under my palm. By the time I reached his cock, his hand was flying up and down. I wrapped my hand around his and slowed his movements.

"Not too fast."

I licked around the tip of his cock, tasting the precum that leaked from the top. My first taste of Brock and it was everything I could have imagined. A bit tangy and very him.

I took over, slowly stroking Brock, while I slid my other hand down below his balls to his crack. When I found the little puckered entrance, I ran my thumb back and forth over his hole, loosening him up for me. I took my hands from his warm body only long enough to pour some of the cool liquid across my fingers. "Come on, Brock, open up for me." I pressed the tip of my finger against his entrance and practically swallowed my tongue when it slipped in easily.

Brock's body was tight and warm, waiting for me. I moved my finger back and forth, letting his body get used to the intrusion. When Brock began to push back on my finger, I twisted my hand, searching for that spongy spot that would make him see stars. I pressed down on it and was rewarded with Brock's shout as it filled the room.

"I never imagined how good that would feel."

I pressed down again. Watching him come apart in front of me made my cock beg for release. With Brock's hips undulating off the bed, I knew he was ready for more. I slipped in another finger. It wasn't long before Brock pressed against my hand, taking two fingers with ease.

By the time I had three fingers deep within Brock, the moaning and grunting echoed through the room. His hand was back on his cock.

"Please, Dec. I'm ready. I need you."

I removed my fingers from his body and relished the low groan that left him. "It won't be long, baby." I ran my tongue down his thigh as I moved back to roll the condom down my length. "Turn over."

Brock rolled onto his stomach. I had to fist the base of my cock to stop myself from coming. Brock naked was a beautiful sight. I ran my fingers down his spine to his ass cheeks. I spread his cheeks apart and lined my cock up with the sexiest hole I'd ever seen. Brock began to fidget below me. I pressed forward, sinking deep into his body. I slowed my movements, giving him a chance to adjust.

"Keep going. I want to feel all of you."

I pressed the rest of the way in, the feel of Brock surrounding me had my head spinning. Needing to move, I pulled back and pressed back in. "Fuck, Brock. So fucking sexy. So tight."

"Do it again," he begged.

I moved back and thrust back home again. My eyes rolled to the back of my head. The lust I'd contained to get Brock ready for me had broken loose. I bit down into Brock's shoulder and braced my arms on either side of his head. "I'm going to make you feel like you never have before."

I held myself high above him and sank deep into his body. Over and over again, I thrust into Brock. He clawed at the sheet. He tried moving his hand below his stomach. The desire to come rode me hard, at least as hard as I was riding Brock. I needed to come, but I wouldn't tip over the edge without him.

I gripped his hips tight and pulled him back until he was on his hands and knees. He reached for his dick, but I knocked his hand out of the way and took him in my palm, stroking at the same pace I pounded into his body.

Brock's cock jerked and his shout filled the room. "Fuck, Brock." I thrust twice more into his body and came harder and longer than I ever had in my life. I held him tight to me as I filled the condom.

When I felt I could move without collapsing on Brock, I let go of his hips. Brock dropped down onto the bed. Wanting to snuggle in next to him like the night before I left, I tugged off the condom and tied off before tossing it into the trash can.

"We should clean up," I said, curling into the warmth of Brock's body.

His eyes were already half closed. "We can tomorrow."

I pressed tighter to him and placed a kiss on his shoulder, then his cheek, and finally his lips.

"Thank you for trusting me."

"No thanks needed. I've always trusted you. Tonight was perfect."

Perfect was the best word to describe it.

Chapter 22

Brock

We parked in Ayden Thompson's driveway but sat for a moment in Declan's car. I didn't want to drive. My nerves had gotten the better of me, and the closer we got to here, the more nervous I felt.

Declan's hand squeezing my knee brought my focus back to him. "We don't have to tell them. I mean it. I don't want to push you." He had to be the kindest, most understanding person on the planet.

When Declan told me about the invitation to the cookout at Ayden and Rome's home, he asked if I wanted to go with him. It was up to me how he would introduce us. We talked about who would be there, only his teammates and their significant others. It was a small gathering.

Declan and I were dating. We were boyfriends.

I hated hiding and this was a small step to me being comfortable in my skin while we were out. We weren't out there where the media could see. It was the perfect way to ease into things. So I agreed. I couldn't resist, not when Declan gave me that dimpled smile I loved so much.

Now we were staring at other cars, the ones his teammates or their partners drove. There was a Ferrari 458, a Mustang GT, and an Aston Martin DB11. Who knew what was behind the closed garage doors? Then there was a Toyota Camry, which didn't seem to fit with the others, just like my Sequoia wouldn't have either.

Placing my hand on top of Declan's, I turned to him. "I want to do this. I want them to know we're not just friends." And I seriously needed to talk to Ethan. I still hadn't told Declan about what his brother asked me to promise, and every day felt like I was lying to the man I was quickly falling for.

I wasn't sure how to handle things. Did I call Ethan and blurt out that I was seeing his brother? Then, doing so would be behind Declan's back. I was sure it was something he'd like to tell Ethan himself. But if he did before I could talk to him, all hell would break loose. Either way, I was screwed. Ethan was going to get mad regardless but the more I thought about it, his reaction wasn't the one I feared most anymore. It was Declan's. How he was going to feel when the truth came out. That I made a promise and because of it, was worried to be out in public with him.

Declan gave me a quick kiss then opened his door to get out. I followed suit. Laughter and the sounds of people talking drifted from the back of the house, so we followed it until we came around and saw a gorgeous yard. There was an in-ground pool with water so clean and calm I wanted to jump right into it. Pavers surrounded it with well-maintained landscaping complementing the area. A pool house sat a little ways back. The pavers led to a big patio with a built-in grill and bar area.

There was an older woman with short brown hair flipping food over the flames. The guys were lounging in chairs or standing in the shade. No one was in the pool currently.

It was Sunday night and these guys had played an afternoon game, which they won. They deserved to rest and relax. I was sure it was hard for them to all get together during the season.

"Declan!" Ayden called and walked over to us. Declan was standing close to me with his hand on the small of my back. It was comforting having that little touch there.

He pulled his hand away to shake Ayden's, who hugged him quick. Then Declan focused on me. "Ayden, this is Brock Richmond."

Ayden and I shook. He had a warm smile. "It's great to meet you. Declan has told us a lot of good things about you." Declan placed his arm around my waist, pulling me gently to his side. Ayden's eyes widened for a split second before that smile turned into a big grin. "So this is the guy who's been making you so happy."

"Yep, and I finally caught him." I could feel my cheeks heat and it wasn't from the strong July sun. "We're just keeping it quiet for a bit, and I know none of you would breathe a word of it outside of here."

"Hell, no. This place is like Vegas. Come on. I want to introduce you two around."

First, I met Callen Teague and his partner, Spencer Matson. I knew who all the players were and had seen their significant others a time or two in the media. Callen and Spencer were both very friendly and not as loud and boisterous as who I met next.

"Oh my, look at you," Evan said as he peered up at me after we were introduced to him. His dark brown hair was a little longer on top and it appeared that he perfected the messy hair look. His blue eyes checked me out from head to toe, causing me to shift from one foot to the other under his scrutiny.

"Easy there, sexy," Vander said as he put his arm around Evan's waist. "Let's not scare away Declan's boyfriend."

"But... but... he's the size of a tree." Evan turned his gaze to Declan. "You're not a small guy either, but tell me... Do you like to climb him? Because I can imagine how much fun that would be. You could wrap your body around him and hold on for the ride."

"Jesus, Ev," Kasper said, coming over. He was someone who needed no introduction. I'd met him when he took over the Sandpipers.

Evan hooked his arm through Kasper's. "You know this big hunk of man meat, don't you?"

"Yes, I do. He was on the Sandpipers. Recently retired." Kasper extended his hand to me. "Nice to see you again, Brock."

"You, too."

"How's retired life treating you?"

Evan's eyes shined brightly. "If I'm reading this right, with the way Declan's leaning into him, it's treating Brock real good."

Kasper merely shook his head. "You'll get used to him."

I chuckled. "It's fine. I don't mind."

Another guy stepped over. He was the same height as Evan, but his hair was light blond and he had striking green eyes. "You say that now," he joked. "Evan's a handful." Before Evan could say anything, the man introduced himself to me as Ayden's husband, Rome, then he greeted Declan.

Evan lightly hip checked Rome, causing him to laugh. Ayden and Marcus joined us. We talked for a bit as meat seared on the grill. I found out from Marcus that his and Kasper's housekeeper, Sylvia, was the one cooking for us tonight. She heard Ayden and Rome were hosting a cookout and wanted to help. He said she loved cooking for others.

Ayden, Marcus, Callen, Vander, and Declan started talking about baseball and ended up drifting closer to the grill where Rome was standing near Sylvia. That left me with Kasper, Evan, and Spencer. They bantered back and forth, obvious to anyone who was near them how close they were.

We took seats, except I sat down a little slower than the others. My knees slightly ached from standing for a while.

"If you don't mind me asking, are you okay?" Spencer inquired.

"Yeah, just years of playing football wore my body out some."

"Has anyone given you exercises to keep your joints moving fluidly?"

"I work out almost every day at home."

"Working out and doing exercises to keep your body moving aren't always the same thing. If you'd like, I can recommend some things for you to do. It will help ease some of your aches and probably make working out better on your body, too."

"Spencer is the doctor of our group," Evan added.

"I'm a physical therapist, not an MD."

He waved him off. "Whatever. Point is, he can help. He knows what he's doing. The Jetties use him."

"Sandpipers now, too," Kasper cut in.

Spencer chuckled. "I've had to increase my staff to keep up with demand. I personally strictly work with the players now. My team handles the other patients who come to the practice and back me up elsewhere when needed."

Kasper clapped a hand on Spencer's shoulder. "We need to clone you."

"What I need is a vacation."

"Soon enough you'll be getting married and off on your honeymoon," Evan said with dreamy eyes then focused on me. "What about you and Declan?"

I let out a nervous laugh. "I don't think we're ready to walk down the aisle."

"Maybe not, but you better lock that man in. Have you seen the way people throw themselves at professional athletes?" He laughed. "Of course, you have. You're one of them."

"No, I'm not. No one ever showed me the attention the players on the Emperors get."

A hand on my shoulder had me turning, finding Declan behind me. He came to my side and propped his hip against my chair. "They didn't know what was hiding behind that helmet all those years." He smiled down at me. He was simply stunning.

"Awww, look how cute they are, Kas." Turning, I found Evan watching us with his chin propped up on his palm. "You should know, I have no boundaries, especially once you're part of our inner circle. You're one of us now. Nothing is off-limits." His words didn't unnerve me like they might have when we first got here.

The more time I spent with these men, the more I got the sense of family from them. They were close friends, comfortable with one another. Here, no one was perceived as better than anyone else. They weren't famous ballplayers, or a billionaire in Kasper's case. They weren't an heir to a fortune like Evan. They were just guys enjoying a night off together.

Sylvia called for everyone to come eat. I stood and was about to walk over when a hand on my arm caused me to pause.

"Can we talk for a moment?" Kasper asked.

I nodded. "Sure." Declan squeezed my hand before joining his friends, leaving me alone with Kasper.

"You're welcome to tell me to go fuck myself and that this isn't any of my business, but did you not feel comfortable coming out when you were on the Sandpipers? The reason I ask is that if there's a problem within the team where either players, coaches, or staff aren't making people feel free to be who they are, I need to address it." This man was truly one of the good ones.

"Nothing like that. I haven't come out to my own parents yet. I was..." It took me a moment to gather my thoughts. I was about to discuss myself with someone I didn't know well, but felt at ease with nonetheless. "I'd always been gay but was scared coming out in high school then college. Once I got to the NFL, I didn't feel it was right to say anything. I didn't want to jeopardize my career. It wasn't just me depending on the money I earned, but my family as well."

"It's not easy coming out, let alone when you're in a sport where it's not always conducive to do so. I like to think I set a standard with the Jetties. I know some of the other teams like to throw insults on the ice when they're playing us. You can imagine the slurs that come from them with me as a gay team owner and having guys on the team who aren't all straight. But the players we have, they appreciate the environment I've created. It's unfortunate more aren't open. Athletes shouldn't feel like their career hinges on their sexual orientation."

I shook my head. "I could have come out, but the fear was always there. Then I was so close to retirement that I knew if I could just hold out a little longer, I could be who I wanted. And now..." I glanced over to where Declan took a seat with a plate piled high with food, leaving the spot next to him open for me. "Now I have to find the courage I lacked for so long. Dec has been amazing, not pushing me. Tonight was a big step for me coming here as his date."

"When you're with us, you're in a safe space."

"I appreciate that more than you know."

"You and I never got a chance to get acquainted before, but I hope we can now. If you ever need someone to talk to, you've got my number. Use it." When Kasper and Tim bought the Sandpipers, they made sure we all knew we were part of their family, and being as such, gave us their personal numbers to contact them any time. Not that I would ever have done so, but I was no longer a player for Kasper's team.

"Thank you."

"When you're ready to come out to more than us, we'll have your back."

I nodded and swallowed thickly, emotion clogging my throat.

Tonight, I was nervous about coming here. I wasn't sure how anyone would react to me and Declan being together. What I found was more than I could have hoped for. These men had formed a tight bond. One of friendship, not only baseball. By Declan joining the Emperors, he didn't just get traded to another team in the MLB. He got traded to a team where he got more than a place to play the game he loved. He gained the kind of friends I'd have been jealous of if I wasn't standing here among them.

Not that Lali and Ethan weren't supportive of me. They were, but this was different. These men had gone through a lot. Callen became the first guy in the MLB to come out as gay. Vander came up to the majors into a team breaking boundaries. Marcus and Ayden both faced the media as straight men who were now bi. They fell in love with men who became their husbands.

Then there was Declan, who didn't hide that he liked both men and women. Who chose me for some crazy reason. Who apparently since he was younger wanted to be with me. I was still blown away by that. I couldn't believe it.

Declan turned until his eyes were locked on mine. A slow smile curved those lips I loved to kiss, and he nodded toward the table. I didn't know how I was going to do it, but I had to make everything right. Declan was worth any hell I had to deal with in regard to Ethan. I just had to hope Declan would be there after everything came out into the open. I wasn't sure what I would do if he wasn't.

Chapter 23

Declan

Walking away from Brock was hard. He'd been nervous the entire ride over. Then, once he finally seemed to relax, Kasper asked to speak with him. Yes, Brock was retired and yes, Kasper was his former boss. I just didn't want any tension to ruin the night we were having. With my plate overflowing with food, I sat down at the table Ayden and Rome had set up, my eyes wandering to Brock to make sure he was all right.

His gaze connected with mine and he smiled. I nodded toward the table, wanting him by my side. Brock turned back to Kasper for a moment, and I felt someone lean against me.

"That looks like a lot more than lust," Ayden whispered in my ear.

I turned to see he'd taken the seat on the other side of me. Serious eyes were locked on mine. Years had passed since Ayden and I shared everything. He was one of the first guys on our college team to know I was bi. Always my roommate for away games, we always talked. Now, even though the time had passed, he could see right through me.

"That's because it is." Our voices were low, keeping our conversation from the rest of the table. Luckily, Evan was commanding almost everyone else's attention with some outrageous story. I glanced over to where Brock and Kasper were filling up their plates. Brock had been my fantasy from the moment I'd figured out I liked men and women, and nothing about that had changed. "I've wanted him longer than I care to admit. He's my brother's best friend, but he's always been more to me. Watching over me, helping me. I love him."

"Have you told him?"

"No." I took one last peek a Brock. "I'm not sure he's ready to hear it yet. I don't want him to feel like he has to come out to everyone for me. This is the first place we've gone as a couple. He needs time and, as long as I have him, I don't want to push him."

"Don't wait too long. The way he looks at you tells me he may be more than ready to hear it, even if he doesn't realize it himself yet."

Brock walked up, effectively ending the conversation. I knew it wouldn't be the last time Ayden brought it up. He'd always wanted the best for his friends, and if that meant me telling Brock exactly how I felt, he'd push until I did. Brock's plate was full, but noticeably smaller than the other athletes at the table.

When everyone had settled down and was focused on their food for a moment, I leaned over and whispered in Brock's ear. "Everything okay?"

"Everything's great." The smile on Brock's face said it all. He may not be comfortable coming out to the world, but he found a place where he could be himself outside of his home, and for that, I was extremely grateful.

"Jesus, Ev."

I looked over to see Kasper shaking his head at Evan, who deep throated a sausage while shooting lust-filled eyes at Vander.

Ayden pointed across the table, moving his finger back and forth between the two of them. "There will be no fucking in my pool or my backyard."

Vander reached for Evan, tracing a line down his Adam's apple. "He just oozes sex, doesn't he?"

A chorus of noes rang out and Evan yanked the sausage out of his mouth. "I'm sexy as hell, thank you very much."

"Not when we have to watch you two fuck in every place we go," Spencer deadpanned.

Evan whipped his head around. "We do not."

"Yes, you do. I've seen more of your ass than I've seen of my own wife's." Coming through the gate was Dominic with a baby in his arms and a woman by his side.

"Filter, Dominic," she said, taking the baby out of his hands. "We've talked about this." And for the first time since I met him, Dominic nodded and zipped his lips.

"I've never seen that before." I chuckled.

Brock's brows drew together, but Callen was quick to fill us in.

"The only person in the world who can control Dominic's mouth is Cheryl. He's always on his best behavior with her or she reminds him to be."

"That has to be the funniest shit I've ever seen."

"At least until tomorrow's game when we pay for him having to bite his tongue today." Callen clasped me on the shoulder, his gaze now on Spencer as he walked over to Cheryl. "Don't worry. You get used to it."

"She's absolutely beautiful," Spencer said, stepping in front of Cheryl. "Can I hold her?"

"Thank you and of course." Cheryl handed over the baby girl. The sun had started to dip toward the horizon, casting a pinkish glow across the sky. Even in the dimmer light, I could see the baby had the same light eyes as her mother.

"Aren't you a cutie," Spencer cooed, gently bouncing the little girl in his arms. Callen got up and walked over to Spencer.

"Of course, she is. She looks like her mommy not her daddy." Callen kept his eyes on Dominic while he played with the baby.

"F—" Dominic started, but Cheryl cut him off.

"Dominic."

Dominic snapped his mouth shut. The glare he shot Callen would have leveled anyone on another team, but Callen laughed him off and turned his attention back to the baby.

Dominic took Cheryl's hand and brought her over to where Brock and I sat at the table. The stiffness in Brock's posture had returned. I knew it was likely to happen with each new person he met. I stood up to greet Dominic and his wife.

"Didn't think you were making it." I held a hand out to Dominic, who took it and pulled me into a hug.

"Who knew getting out of the house with a baby took so much time?" He let go of me and turned to the woman beside him. "Cheryl, this is the newbie of the team, Declan. Declan, this is the goddess of my life, Cheryl. And the ass—" Cheryl gave him a warning glare. "Callen is fawning over our princess, Kailey."

I held my hand out to Cheryl, who stepped up and gave me a warm hug. "Ignore Dominic. He forgets how to behave sometimes." Just the thought of how Cheryl would react if she saw the way Dominic acted in the locker room had a bubble of laughter rising up.

I swallowed it down. "I'm sure you do everything you can."

"It's definitely a full-time job."

"I bet it is. Your daughter is beautiful."

"Thank you. She's definitely a handful, like her father." She glanced up at Dominic. The love between the two of them was obvious. He gazed down at his wife like she hung the moon. I had to wonder if I looked at Brock that way because I felt it deep down into my soul.

I placed my hand on his shoulder. Brock was quick to stand and face the two new arrivals. "Dominic and Cheryl, this is my boyfriend, Brock Richmond."

Dominic laughed and reached out a hand to Brock. "So another guy playing for your team, huh, Callen?" he called out over his shoulder.

"Actually, pretty sure he plays for my team." Marcus passed by with Kasper at his side and a plate full of food.

"He's right. Boys, girls, I like them all. No one compares to Brock, though."

Brock took his hand. "I'm the one who plays for Callen's team." I couldn't believe Brock had said that, which only showed me his comfort level growing around my friends and teammates.

While they shook hands, Dominic studied Brock's face. I hadn't introduced him to anyone as a retired Sandpiper. As his former boss, Kasper knew. I didn't want Brock to feel like he had to live up to any expectations of himself when he was in the NFL, which was completely ridiculous considering at least half of the people at the barbecue were professional athletes.

Dominic snapped his fingers in the air as soon as he figured it out. "Brock Richmond. You played for the Sandpipers." Dominic looked to where Kasper and Marcus sat eating. "Kasper, he's one of your players."

Marcus rolled his eyes. "Well, aren't you observant tonight? Pretty sure my husband knows who works for him and who doesn't."

Dominic flipped Marcus off behind Cheryl's back.

"Actually, former player," Brock cut in "I retired at the end of the season."

Dominic frowned. "Shame. Tim and Kasper are just starting to breathe life back into the team."

"They are. But my body was not on board with waiting for that. I'll be happy to cheer them on from the stands."

"Brock, you're always welcome to watch from our box," Kasper offered.

"I appreciate it."

Dominic led Cheryl over to the table to make a plate. Having seen plenty of parents running around, chasing their kids, it had to be nice to have a minute to eat peacefully while other people played with their daughter.

"Oh my god, she's adorable." I glanced behind me to see Rome practically bouncing in his seat.

Ayden wrapped his arm around Rome's shoulder. "You can hold Kailey if you want. Cheryl would absolutely be okay with it."

Rome's eyes widened. "What if I drop her?" He shook his head emphatically. "I can't." Ayden took Rome's hand and helped him up from his seat. "Where are we going?"

"We'll hold her together."

Ayden walked Rome up to Spencer and Kailey. Ayden held his arms out. "May I?"

Kailey reached for Ayden and Spencer smiled, placing her in Ayden's arms. Spencer took Callen's hand as they walked back to the table whispering to each other. I couldn't take my eyes from the way Ayden held Kailey, pulling Rome in so they could hold her together. Rome's posture was stiff at first until he slowly relaxed with Kailey, eventually moving into his arms.

The two of them together were sweet. The way Ayden cared for and looked out for Rome proved how much he truly loved him. My gaze moved back to Brock. I wanted that with him. That connection. The shared desire for each other. I'd told Brock that I wanted us to be exclusive. Just the two of us. Now, I just needed to get up the courage to tell him I loved him. Ayden was right. There was no point in not telling him how I felt. Maybe Brock was more ready to hear it than I thought.

Tonight was a big step in the direction of Brock being comfortable in his own skin outside of the house.

Hopefully, someday Brock would be ready to be out with me in the world.

Before we got to that point, I needed to get up the nerve to talk to Ethan. Even if Brock was his best friend, I knew that wouldn't be enough to spare him from Ethan's big brother tactics. He wanted the best for me, and I had to hope eventually he would see that Brock was it. Maybe I was a chicken for not telling him sooner, but until I was sure Brock was comfortable with all of this, there didn't seem to be a point in crossing that bridge just yet.

We stayed for a while longer. Laughing, eating, and joking. It was great to get to know my teammates' significant others in such a relaxed setting. Since today's game was the last before the All-Star break and a few of us needed to travel tomorrow for the game, we called it a night, but I had a feeling this wouldn't be the last time we were all together.

I handed Brock the keys as we walked to the car. I wasn't drunk, but I'd definitely had more to drink than him. Through the entire night, I'd only seen him have one beer.

"You drive."

He nodded and took the keys, walking around to the driver's side while I climbed in the passenger side. Brock started the car and turned out of the drive. Ayden lived in the opposite direction of the beach, making the ride to Brock's house longer than anyone else's.

I reached over and laid my hand on his thigh. He'd need his free hand to shift gears. "Did you have fun tonight?"

"I was nervous at first, but it was nice to finally be myself around other people."

"I'm glad." I watched the road in front of us for a minute before looking at Brock again. "You know you could've held the baby tonight."

"I'm not sure I'm really the baby holding type." I chuckled. "What are you laughing at?" He glanced over at me for a second before gazing back to the road.

"Every day I learn how much we actually agree on. Not really the baby holding type either."

In the dim light of the dash, I could see his smile. "That's a good thing to know."

It really was. I settled into the seat, content to watch Brock as he drove home. I truly believed we could have what everyone else at the barbecue had. The closeness, the relationship. The love. I only needed to be patient and let Brock take things at his pace. Eventually, he'd be ready to introduce us to the world.

Chapter 24

Brock

"I'm in love with him." There, I said it. Not to Declan. No, that would make sense. Today, I was confessing my feelings for Declan to Lali. I dropped my head into my hands. Lali's gentle touch caused me to raise my gaze to hers. Her hair was down in the back but pulled up on the sides to keep it out of her face. Her white T-shirt was hanging off one shoulder, revealing the electric blue tank top beneath.

"It's okay."

"It's not. I should be out in public walking hand in hand with Dec. Instead, I'm hiding our relationship."

I thought back to the dinner on Sunday with some of Declan's teammates and their significant others. It was so nice to be myself. To let my issues fall to the side and just be authentic.

"You need to talk to him." She said what I already knew. Talking to Lali would only get me so far. Declan was the one who should be sitting across from me. "I know you're worried about Ethan, but you have to ask yourself what's more important right now. Your relationship with Declan or Ethan?"

"Why can't I have both?"

"I think you can, but it may take a bit to get there. From all you've told me, Ethan isn't going to be happy you're sleeping with his brother. He's your friend, though. If he cares about you and Declan, then he'll eventually realize you two being together is right."

"What if it rips our families apart?"

She cocked an eyebrow at me.

I groaned.

I had so many fears where this was concerned: losing Declan, losing Ethan, not having the family connection between the Richmonds and the Armitages.

"Do you want more to eat?" Lali asked, changing the subject as she got up from the table. We were in her kitchen eating at the small table she had there. Living downtown like she did, her place was on the smaller and more expensive side. But it was perfect for her.

"No, I'm good. Thank you for feeding me." She was a good cook. Her company was even better.

After we cleared the table and cleaned the dishes, we went to her living room and sat down on the couch.

Lali curled her legs under herself and faced me. "I can see how much this is eating at you. You're at this point in your life where you finally have someone you love, and you can't enjoy it like you should. I hate that for you. I wish it wasn't this difficult to be with Declan."

"I'm making it harder than it needs to be. It's so easy when it's just the two of us. I feel like it's going to crash down around me soon. I'm waiting for the other shoe to drop."

"You need to talk to Declan. You have to come clean."

"I know. When he finds out what I promised Ethan, how that's the real reason I've been keeping us at home, he might leave."

"You don't know that."

She was right in the fact that I didn't know it for certain, but I had a strong feeling about it. I omitted the truth from Declan. I didn't share what Ethan had said. What I was doing was wrong. The lies, the guilt, the weight on my shoulders... It all had to stop. But when it did, everything would go with it. In the two months since Declan started staying with me, he'd become my entire world. And I was on the cusp of possibly losing him.

Lali took my hand in hers and gave it a gentle squeeze. "Two things, then we can go out for ice cream." She knew me all too well. With the hot July sun, I'd been craving something sweet. I didn't keep much junk food in my house, but there was a great little place around the corner from Lali we loved going to.

"One," she began, "no matter what happens, you'll always have me. I'm not going anywhere. Two, being in love means laying your heart out there for another person to take. With it, you run the risk of them destroying it. But you also take a chance on them holding it close and cherishing it as much as you do theirs. If you're truly meant to be with Declan, this will work out. You have to have faith."

"You know I'm not religious."

She rolled her eyes dramatically. "And you know I'm not either. I didn't specify faith in what, just believe that you're on the path you're meant to be on. You'll get to where you should be."

"Is that supposed to comfort me, because it's lacking."

Releasing my hand, she playfully shoved my shoulder, only I didn't move because Lali was much smaller than me. I gripped her hand and pulled her in for a hug. "Thank you for being here for me," I whispered.

"Always. You're my best friend, Brock. One of my only friends if I think about it."

I chuckled. "You have a lot of friends. Plus, there's a whole football team of guys who would help you if you ever needed anything."

"Acquaintances is what they are."

Lali was one of those people who didn't let many in to truly know her. I was sure she could have had a legion of friends, but instead she kept them at arm's length. I was glad she let me in.

We spent a little while longer talking before we went and got ice cream. We sat at a little round table near the window, looking out at the people walking by. It was Friday and the streets were bustling with the rush of people heading home after work for the weekend.

I took the long way back to my house, winding through the city, not minding the traffic for once. I needed the time to think. To reflect on how I felt about Declan. Everything would change tonight after I confessed. I had to do it. Had to get this weight off me.

Declan wouldn't be back until late since his game started just after seven. I was in no rush to be home alone with Sampson. I used to love the silence, now I loved the sound of another person in my home. Of Declan being there and filling the space with his voice and laughter. With his warmth and care.

Hours passed while I cleaned counters that were already clean. While I vacuumed, folded laundry, and did basically anything to get my mind off the talk I needed to have with Declan. There was no way for us to move forward unless it was all out in the open.

It was late when the door to the house opened, and Declan stepped through. I steeled myself as I stood and walked over to greet him. I had to do this.

My stomach knotted, those butterflies that were usually there when he was around disappeared out of fear. My hands shook. I couldn't remember the last time I was so frightened, and not in the scary movie type of way but the type where I could lose the man I loved. The man I never said those words to. I couldn't until he knew the truth.

Before any words slipped past my lips, Declan was in my arms with his lips against mine. Every thought fled my mind as I sank into the feel of him. He pulled back only a breath and only long enough to take my hand in his and pull me up the stairs, where he kicked my bedroom door shut. Or should I say ours. Ever since the first night we had sex, Declan had been sleeping in bed with me when he wasn't on the road. It was everything I wanted. I loved having him close.

"I want you to top me," Declan said between kisses, surprising me.

I moaned deep in my throat at the thought of being buried inside him. Every time we'd been together since the first one, I'd bottomed for Declan. I loved it, couldn't get enough.

Now, with the thought of being inside him, I realized how much I missed that and wanted it. I loved giving up control to him, but I was open to taking a turn at driving things.

We stumbled through the room, shedding our clothes until we both fell onto the bed in a tangle of limbs. Declan was on top of me, his weight a welcome presence, grounding me, keeping me in this moment, which was what I needed.

In the back of my mind there was a little nagging voice, reminding me I wanted to talk to him, but I gave that voice the finger and promised I'd do it later. Right now, I needed this man like I needed air to breathe.

Our dicks rubbed together as Declan ground down against me. But it wasn't enough. I needed more.

I slapped around for the nightstand drawer to pull out a condom and lube. Tossing the condom on the bed, I reached for the lube, flicking the cap open and spreading it on my fingers. I rubbed it around to get it warm before reaching behind Declan as he spread his legs for me. He didn't let up humping against me. It was driving me closer to the edge, but I wanted to finish inside him.

With one finger, I gently breached him and took a moment for him to get adjusted to it. I didn't know how much he'd bottomed before me. I wanted to make it good for him, even if every part of my being was screaming to get inside him.

Declan took over and slid back so my full finger went inside him. He let out a low moan and tipped his head back, exposing the column of his throat. Leaning up, I licked and sucked on his neck, loving the taste of his skin.

"Need another," he told me.

I complied, slipping a second finger inside him. I worked in and out of him, crooking my fingers, searching for the spot that would send pleasure through his body. I knew when I found it because his body jerked, a drop of precum seeping from the tip of his dick. Reaching down with my free hand, I swiped it up and brought it to my lips. Delicious.

With him writhing above me, I added a third finger. I had to make sure I didn't hurt him when I finally breached him with my dick. I kept a slow, steady pace, stretching him with my fingers.

"No more," he told me. "I need you."

I quickly rolled the condom on then moved us so I was over him, with his legs bent near his chest. Thank god for flexible ballplayers. I lubed up my dick and with my eyes latched on his, slowly entered him. I had to fight everything in me to keep my eyes open. They wanted to shut, to soak in the pleasure of his tight body squeezing me. Declan's eyes remained open as well, his mouth slack as he breathed through me moving farther into him.

When his body went lax under me, I knew he was comfortable, so I started to move. With slow, languid thrusts, I took him over and over. I held his legs, kept him open for me, as I peered down and watched myself enter him. It was better than any porn I watched. Better than anything I could have thought of in my fantasies.

Declan angled his hips but couldn't seem to find what he was searching for. I reached for a pillow to prop his waist up. He cried out when I found my rhythm with the new angle. His hand went to his dick so he could stroke himself. I batted his hand away to take over. I wanted to have control tonight. I wanted his pleasure to be done by my hand.

He was like velvet-coated steel in my palm as I stroked him. His moans were whispers as his breath skated over my skin. I was hovering just above him. I needed to be close. Needed to feel every inch of him. If he'd been on his stomach, I would have wrapped my body around him and humped into him as best I could. I couldn't get enough.

I wished the condom wasn't between us. I wanted to claim him, mark him as mine, and that was so unlike me. I was jealous over other guys near Declan, sure, but this need roared to life in me that I had to make him mine in every possible way.

Declan called out my name as he came. It was the combination of that and this raw need in me for him that pushed me over the edge. I jerked inside him, trying to go as deep as possible until there was nothing left in me.

I finally collapsed down on top of him for a few beats of my heart before moving to roll off. I had to be crushing him with my weight.

Then his arms were there, wrapping around me, holding me tight before I got far. "Not yet."

I tucked my face into his neck as hot tears stung my eyes. This man was everything I'd ever wanted, and he accepted me for who I was, how I looked, every single piece of me.

The words of love were on the tip of my tongue, but I held them in. I'd say them soon. There was only so long I could withhold my feelings from him.

Chapter 25

Declan

The smoky scent of bacon hit my nose before I even reached the bottom of the stairs. Brock was always an early riser. Not me. Not unless we had an early game. Then, after last night's activities, an extra hour of sleep was definitely on the menu. Even though I told him many times he didn't have to wait for me for breakfast, he always did. I'd never deny how much I loved when it was just me and him in the morning. No matter what time of the day I had a game, we always had the mornings. Even if this breakfast was a little later.

At the stove, Brock stood with his back to me, flipping the bacon in the pan, while Sampson sat dutifully by his side waiting to see if a piece might land on the floor for him. Quietly, I walked up behind him and wrapped my arms around his waist. He stiffened in my hold for a brief moment before relaxing.

"Good morning." I pressed a kiss to the space between his shoulder blades.

He set the tongs down and turned in my arms. His lips were warm and tasted like coffee when he pressed them to mine. "Good morning. Sit and I'll bring breakfast over."

I settled down carefully in the seat at the counter. My ass was deliciously sore. It had been a bit since I'd had a man take me the way Brock did last night. I'd deal with a sore ass to have him do it to me again and again. Coffee and a shower would take care of everything.

The more I watched Brock, the more I knew something was off. I couldn't put my finger on it. We had breakfast together every morning unless I was on the road. This was different. He seemed to be on edge. I knew he topped when he had been with other men. We hadn't switched until last night. His movements were stiff and cautious. Whatever was on his mind, I hoped he'd talk to me about it. I thought we'd broken through these barriers when we had the conversation about being exclusive. Apparently, I'd been wrong.

Brock set two plates overflowing with bacon and omelets on the counter. He turned back to the fridge and pulled out the orange juice, filling two glasses. With glasses and mugs of coffee in front of us, we started in on our meals. Our normal conversation was missing throughout, and the weird silence was killing me. I turned in my seat to ask Brock what was going on when my phone went off at the same time as his. I looked at Brock and grabbed my cell.

Ethan.

I swiped open the message to see it was sent to both of us.

Ethan: Got Monday off. Gonna come down and spend it with you two. Want to see Declan play and hang out with Brock. Be there around noon.

I glanced at Brock, who was looking at his own phone. Well, shit. The last thing I wanted was Ethan and Brock in the same house, not if I wanted to be in Brock's bed at night. Noon meant he'd be here in a little over an hour. My phone buzzed again.

Brock: Looking forward to it.

Brock looked up at me. "Can you get tickets for tonight's game?"

"I can. But that's the last thing I'm worried about. Remember we agreed to keep this to ourselves for now. I don't want to deal with Big Brother Ethan. We both know how he'll get when I tell him I'm seeing someone and that someone is his best friend."

"I know." Brock reached out and covered my hand with his. "I think we should—"

I cut Brock off mid-sentence. It sounded like we were on the same page. We usually were, why not this time? "We should go back to separate bedrooms while he's here? I was thinking the same thing." I wiped my lips with the napkin. "We don't have long until he gets here. I'm going to get all of my stuff out of your room before I have to head to the stadium." He started to say something, but I gave him a quick kiss on his lips, then I darted up the stairs to his room.

Brock and I needed to talk to Ethan together, but with only an hour until Ethan arrived, we didn't have time to plan. My brother always wanted the best for me and with the right explanation, he'd see Brock was that man. He loved Brock like a brother, that wasn't the problem. The problem was me. Every decision I made he questioned and analyzed then evaluated some more. He'd see that Brock was the best for me, but how much would he put us through until he got to that point?

It hadn't been easy convincing Brock that we were right for each other. I wasn't willing to risk Ethan's bullshit scaring him back to the point that he didn't think we should be together. I walked into Brock's bedroom and looked around. It was unlikely that Ethan would be in here, but I also couldn't very well walk into his room while Ethan was here if I forgot something.

I shoved my razor and shaving cream into my toiletry bag. My toothbrush and toothpaste were next. When I was sure I had all of my stuff from the bathroom, I set the small bag on the bed and gathered my clothes from the night before. Luckily, I hadn't moved any of my clothes into Brock's room. Usually, I grabbed whatever I planned on wearing the next day from the drawers in the guest room.

With all my stuff safely back in the room I slept in when I first arrived, I called the Emperors' office to set aside two tickets for that night's game. They would leave them at the ticket window for Brock and Ethan to pick up when they got to the stadium. They'd have a few hours together before the game would begin.

I glanced around the room that seemed so unfamiliar to me. For weeks, I'd slept here, but now Brock's room felt like home. It was only one weekend that I needed to deal with sleeping alone.

The time on the bedside table clock told me there were about fifteen minutes until Ethan arrived. If I had any chance of getting out of the house in time to make it to the stadium, I needed to have my stuff packed when he arrived.

Loud laughter reached my ears as I stepped out of the guest room, reminding myself it was only two nights away from Brock. We could do this. Monday night we'd figure out exactly what we could say to Ethan to keep him from putting our relationship through his rigorous evaluation that everything else in my life had gone through. My brother was amazing. Always there for me. Always on my side, cheering me on. Yet, there were times I wished he wasn't so protective. Let me make my own mistakes. That he was just my brother.

"Declan, get your ass down here!"

Times like right now when it was one brother visiting another. Where we could laugh over my screwups and figure out a way to fix them. Instead, he tried to find the problems and solve them first.

"Coming," I called as I bounded down the stairs, my bag on my shoulder.

I barely made it to the bottom of the stairs before Ethan's arms wrapped around me in a giant bear hug. "Missed you," he said, rocking me back and forth.

I patted him on the back. "Missed you too, but soon I'm gonna miss breathing."

Ethan chuckled and let me go. Out of the corner of my eye, I saw Brock leaning against the back of the couch, his hands stuffed into his pockets and one ankle crossed over the other. While his smile was genuine, his posture was tight and rigid. Similar to this morning only worse.

"How's Espen treating you?"

I pulled my focus from Brock and turned to Ethan. "Pretty good. It's nice playing with Ayden again."

Ethan stepped over and wrapped his arm around Brock's shoulder. I noticed him stiffen even more, but I didn't think Ethan realized it. I'd grown so attuned to every move he made that I noticed it instantly. "And is this guy treating you okay?"

The little food still left in my stomach soured. I hated lying to my brother and, even though it wasn't an outright lie, but a lie of omission, I still felt shitty as I said, "He's been great." I dropped my bag and went to the fridge to grab a bottle of water. Anything to keep from letting my brother see the guilt written all over my face.

I tipped my head back to drink. The water in my stomach didn't help the queasy feeling. I needed to get out of here and find a way to get a grip on myself. Two days, I reminded myself. Only two days, then Brock and I would find a way to tell him about us.

When I turned back around, Brock and Ethan had moved to sit on the couch. I followed them over but didn't dare sit down. Brock sat on one end of the U-shaped sofa and Ethan on the other. Sitting in the middle felt weird, like being pulled in two different directions.

"What's it like playing with the Emperors? Rumors are the owner is fucking cool as hell." Ethan propped one leg on his knee. "Takes real good care of his players."

"Tim's great. Rooms on the road are way better than any I stayed in with the Backfins, and Tim makes it a habit during home games to bring a player or two up to his suite to congratulate them on a game well played. It's nice to hear from more than just the manager."

Ethan bobbed his head up and down. "Good, good. And the rest of the team?"

"Love playing with them. They don't treat each other just like teammates. It's more like a family." I picked my bag up. "I gotta get to the stadium. Hang out more tomorrow?"

"Definitely. You have a late game, right, and off on Monday?"

"Yeah. Maybe we can all hit the beach on Monday before you head home?"

"That's what I'm thinking." He moved his gaze to Brock. "You up for the beach Monday?"

Brock shifted in his seat and nodded. "Sounds good." Brock looked at me. "Did you get the tickets?"

Something in his eyes made my chest tighten. *Soon enough.* Soon enough we could be together and not have to worry about anything. The whole world would know that Brock was mine and I was his.

"Yeah, they'll be at the ticket office waiting for you. Down the first base line, near right." I winked. "I'll see you when I get home?" I asked Ethan.

Ethan chuckled. "Maybe. Depends on what time you get back. Some of us work early hours and don't stay up all night. If not, I'll see you in the morning." I turned toward the door when Ethan called my name. "Been a while since I've seen you play in person. Can't fucking wait."

"I'll do my best."

I grabbed the doorknob and stepped out into the humid summer air. The weight on my chest lifted slightly. Tonight, I couldn't focus on what I told my brother and what I hadn't. I had a job to do and that was play the best game I could.

I climbed into the front seat of my car and started toward the stadium. The entire ride there I focused on pushing the problems with my brother and Brock out of my head. There would be time for that tomorrow.

Chapter 26

Brock

This day went downhill fast, and I didn't mean because Ethan was visiting, but at the speed in which it all happened. One moment, I was eating breakfast with Declan, trying to work up the courage to talk to him about his brother, and the next thing I knew, Ethan was texting saying he was on his way for the weekend.

Three days.

With Ethan.

In the same house as Declan.

Who I was completely in love with.

And keeping something from.

If this wasn't a recipe for disaster, I didn't know what was.

Once Declan left, I showed Ethan to the guest room he'd be using. He'd stayed here before, but usually in the room his brother was occupying.

Ethan dropped his bag on the bed. "Did you get more books?"

"I get books all the time, although I think I added a new bookshelf since the last time you were here."

"I knew something was different." He walked over and clasped my shoulder. "Damn, it's good to see you. It's been too long."

I smiled. Hanging out with Ethan was always easy, except when I was hiding something from him. He was like a brother to me. "You've been working nonstop, superstar."

He rolled his eyes. "I know. That's why I knew as soon as I got Monday off, I had to head here. They couldn't ask me to work if I wasn't there. Plus, I want to see Declan play for the Emperors in person. The TV isn't the same."

"No, it's not."

Sampson ambled into the room. Ethan dropped to a knee to scratch the dog's head. A big, wet tongue came out to lick Ethan's chin as a thank you. "I bet you love having your daddy home full time, don't you?" Ethan had the baby voice down pat and Sampson soaked up the attention.

We had some time to kill before we headed to the game, so Ethan and I went down to the beach, came back for lunch, watched some TV, and just caught up with one another. I did everything I could to avoid talking about Declan but since he was a common factor between Ethan and me now, we kept drifting back to him. Luckily, Ethan didn't once bring up my promise to him.

With every word Ethan spoke, my guilt only amplified. I got myself into this situation, but I couldn't say anything to Ethan until I spoke with Declan first. He was the one I needed to talk to, yet he wasn't the one in front of me right now.

After a light dinner, knowing we'd snack at the stadium, we got into my SUV and drove through traffic. Once I parked in the lot and killed the engine, Ethan turned to me. He had a serious look on his face, and I swore my heart was up in my throat. Did he know? Did we miss something at the house and somehow Ethan knew Declan was sleeping in my bed every night?

"Before we get out, I just want to say thank you."

I swallowed so hard I was surprised Ethan didn't hear it. "For what?" Surely he wasn't going to thank me for just how well I was treating his brother.

He grinned. "For being there for Declan, of course. You didn't have to open your home to him, but you did and I'm grateful. I wouldn't have felt nearly as comfortable if he was sleeping at someone else's place or a hotel all this time."

"You're family. I'll always be here for all of you."

"I know, man. That's what makes you a great best friend. I couldn't have asked for someone better in my life."

A great best friend. Was I really when I broke the promise I made to him?

It took everything in me to hold in that I was in love with his brother. Why couldn't Ethan have shown up after I confessed everything to Declan?

Instead of replying, I lightly shoved his shoulder and got out of the SUV. I couldn't stay in there any longer. It was like the air was being sucked from it and I was about to start gasping for breath.

Ethan came around the hood laughing and slung his arm over my shoulders. He was the same height as Declan which meant he was an inch shorter than me, easy enough for him to walk with his arm on me like it was. His brown hair was getting mussed in the slight breeze and those hazel eyes of his reminded me of Declan. But the height, hair, and eyes were where the similarities between them ended.

The brothers were different in a lot of ways. Ethan was broader and more muscled than Declan. Ethan would sometimes get this serious edge to him I never saw his brother have. I guessed that was because of the line of work Ethan was in. Declan had an infectious smile, one that could light up a room. And it did me in every time I saw it.

We stood in line at the ticket window. My mind was stuck on Declan, much like it always was lately. I loved him far beyond anything I could have imagined. It was going to be torturous not having him in bed with me tonight. I wasn't sure how I was going to sleep without him there. When he was on the road, it sucked, but I knew he wasn't in the next room where I couldn't touch him like I wanted to. Hold him while we both drifted off to sleep.

Ethan bumped his shoulder with mine. "I don't think I've ever seen that smile before."

I quickly steeled my features. "What smile?"

"The one that tells me you have someone special in your life and you're thinking about him."

I was a terrible human being for keeping this from my best friend, but I couldn't deny the existence of a person in my life, even if I couldn't tell him it was his brother who made me happier than I'd ever been before. "I do."

We were second in line now and I wanted the people in front of me to move faster so this conversation with Ethan would end.

"Do I get to hear about him?"

I hated this because I really wanted him to see how happy I was. See it written as plain as day on my face how in love I was with his brother. "I haven't even told him how I feel yet."

"I get it. You want him to hear it first. But I can tell you're happy, Brock. You deserve it more than anyone I know."

I ducked my head, sure there was a blush rushing to my cheeks. "Thanks."

"How can I help you?" a woman asked. I hadn't even noticed we were next in line.

We claimed our tickets then made our way into the stadium, first grabbing drinks and snacks before sitting down. Once Declan was on the field, I knew I wouldn't want to leave for a while.

Our seats were right where Declan said they'd be. We settled in to watch the game, but my eyes were always on Declan when they could be. At least if Ethan caught where my gaze was, he wouldn't think anything of it outside of me rooting for his brother.

By the time we got home, I was exhausted. Not physically, mentally. Ethan tried getting more information out of me during the game about the person I was seeing. All I told him was that it was still fairly new, and I hadn't even come out to my parents yet. I needed to do that.

I crawled into bed after showering, sure Ethan would be doing the same. I'd ate too much junk food, more than I normally did. But it wasn't every day one of my best friends was in town. It was good to splurge every now and then.

Time ticked by as I tossed and turned, waiting for Declan to come home so I knew he was safe. Eventually, I gave up and crept downstairs to wait for him. Ethan was sound asleep. I heard his quiet snores when I tiptoed past his room. He was someone who slept like the dead unless he was on call for work. Here, he didn't have to worry about that. He could relax and get the sleep I knew he needed and deserved.

The longer I waited, the more my guilt grew. I had to talk to him. I had to get everything out in the open. It was long past due. I felt like I was going to burst by the time he came through the door.

Sampson was there waiting for him. Declan sat his bag down and quietly shut and locked the door before greeting him. I cleared my throat, the room dark, causing Declan to jump.

"Jesus, Brock, did you need to scare me?" he whisper-yelled.

"Would it have been better if I stepped out of the shadows like a creeper?"

"No, but for fuck's sake." He came over to stand in front of me. His hands went to my hips and his lips met mine.

For a moment I was able to forget everything else. It was just Declan and me in our own little world. He was all I wanted, all I needed.

He pulled back first. "Ethan asleep?"

"Yeah, he's out."

"Good." He took my hand in his and pulled me over to the couch. The lights were out but the curtains were open, letting the moon cast its glow into the room. The only sound was the soft whir of the ceiling fan and the air-conditioning cycling on.

Declan gently pushed my shoulders down until I sat on the couch then he straddled my lap. My dick immediately took interest. Anytime Declan was this close to me, it was game on. Only, I couldn't let that happen right now.

Lips trailed along my neck as Declan pulled at the waistband of the cotton shorts I slept in. Reaching down, I stopped him with my hand on his wrist. He sat up, his eyes meeting mine.

I swallowed hard, much like I did earlier in my SUV. "We need to talk."

Declan slid from my lap to sit next to me. He was turned so he could face me, but I was looking out the sliding door, unsure of how to do this. How to say what I needed to when fear was gripping my throat.

"Okay." His fingers laced with mine. "Whatever it is, we'll get through it." How I hoped that was true.

"I'm going to start at the beginning. When Ethan first called me to see if you could stay here, he asked me something."

"Which was?"

"Let me get it all out and then you can ask anything you want, and I'll answer truthfully. Just please hear me out."

He nodded.

"Ethan knows I'm gay. Knows I don't date ever, but now that I'm retired, he also knows I want to get out there and meet someone. Then he called with news of you being traded to the Emperors and I offered for you to stay here. It was easy and required no thought. You're family, always have been. But then he asked me to make a promise."

I swallowed again as I tried to keep my voice from shaking. "He asked me to keep my hands off you. I said just because we both like men doesn't mean we'll fall into bed together. Then I told him I wanted to hit him for even saying that. That I shouldn't have to make any such promise. He's known me long enough but yet, that's what he wanted and what I gave him. I said I would keep my hands off you. I told him I was his best friend, and he could trust me."

Turning, I locked my eyes with Declan's. Even in the darkened room I could see the firm set of his jaw. Tears built in my eyes. I hated this. "I didn't know when you came here that we'd start something up. I've never wanted to be with someone like I have with you. With every day that's passed, every moment we spent together, I didn't know how to tell you. I felt like I was betraying both you and Ethan. I knew I had to tell you but have been worried about what you'd say, so I kept telling myself I'd tell you soon, work up the courage to do so. With Ethan here... I couldn't put it off any longer."

Declan shook off my hand and crossed his arms. I waited for him to say something, but he remained silent.

"Dec, please understand. I didn't know at the time something would develop between us. I'd never intentionally hurt you."

Chapter 27

Declan

The back of my neck burned. I needed to get up and move around. If I thought I could yell and not wake up Ethan, I would have. How could Brock keep shit like that from me? Made me wonder what else was he hiding. What else he'd talked to Ethan about when it came to me, besides the fact that we were fucking.

He promised me he would never talk to Ethan about me or what I was doing. Yet, they'd had an entire conversation about whether or not Brock was allowed to fuck me. Who in the hell were they to decide where I did or didn't stick my dick?

I couldn't stay still any longer. I had to get out of here, get some fresh air. But there was something I had to know first. Standing up, I faced Brock.

"Why didn't you mention this when we talked about the reasons for keeping this—" I moved my finger back and forth between the two of us. "—between us?" My voice came out quiet and calm. Not what I expected. I was proud of myself for keeping it together when I wanted to yell and scream and throw a fit.

I didn't know who to be more pissed at—Ethan or Brock. Both assholes trying to decide what was best for me, without asking me what I wanted. I wasn't a fucking kid anymore.

Brock's eyes dropped to the floor for a moment, then rose to meet mine. Even in the dim light from the moon, I could see the regret there. It just wasn't enough to dissipate the anger in the moment. "I knew you'd be mad that I made the promise. I didn't want to lose you."

"And you thought lying through omission was the way to not make me mad?"

I couldn't keep going. I needed air.

Needed to get out of here.

I spun on my heel and stormed toward the door, swiping my keys off the kitchen counter as I went.

"Dec, wait," Brock called out. I stopped with my hand on the knob. "Let's talk about this."

Without turning around, I unlocked the door and pulled it open. "No."

I didn't wait for a response, just shut the door behind me and bounded down the stairs to my car.

If I stayed here, either we'd wake Ethan up, and I wasn't ready to face him yet, or Brock would keep wanting to talk. Something I didn't feel like doing yet. I yanked opened the driver's door and climbed inside.

My hands shook as I tugged my phone from my pocket to text Ayden. I thought about it for a split second before I started typing. I wanted to talk, but not to Brock. I had to work out my own feelings first.

Me: Are you still up?

It took a moment, but the answer came through.

Ayden: Yeah. Everything okay?

Me: Not really. Can I come over?

Ayden: You know you're always welcome here.

Not bothering to respond, I dropped the phone on the passenger seat and backed out of the garage. For the first time since arriving at Brock's place two months ago, it felt good to drive away from it—a place I'd considered home up until then. Now, the anger and hurt surrounded me until it was suffocating. I couldn't breathe, couldn't think sitting in the same room as him.

With Ayden living outside the city, it gave me time to calm down. To look at the entire situation. Even then, there seemed to be no good reason for Ethan and Brock to meddle in my fucking life like I was a goddamn toddler.

I reached Ayden's gate and punched in the code he'd given me, taking the drive to the house. I'd barely stepped foot out of the car when the front door opened and Ayden stood there, the light filtering around him.

I walked up, the cool air from inside teasing me. The anger had thrummed through my veins so soundly, I hadn't noticed the heat on my skin. Now that the storm had calmed a bit, I felt the beads of sweat forming at the base of my neck and on my brow.

Ayden didn't bother asking a question. He simply reached out and pulled me into a hug. If there was one person in this city who would be able to understand and talk me through this, it was Ayden. Sure, I could have hit the bar and gotten myself drunk before going home, but I knew that never solved the problem. It only pushed it off for a little while until I had to face it in the morning, along with a colossal hangover.

"Come in." He brought me inside to the living room, where Rome sat with his legs curled under him on the opposite sofa.

I stopped short. "I'm sorry. I didn't mean to interrupt."

"You didn't." Rome patted the couch beside him. "If you want, I can go upstairs."

"You don't have to leave."

Rome waved me over. "Then come sit. What happened?"

Rome had to be one of the kindest men I'd ever met. Like Ayden, he did what he could to make the others around him happy. He wanted the best for people and would find a way to make that happen. I took the seat next to Rome where he continued to point. Ayden took the one across from us.

I leaned forward and rested my elbows on my knees. "Not sure I told you, but my brother, Ethan, is in town for the weekend."

"Shit," Ayden mumbled. He knew I loved my brother; how close we were. But he also knew that my brother's caring, overprotective ways could push me over the edge. This was one of those times. Except, this time, Ethan had gone way past the line of overprotectiveness and straight into the land of assholery.

Rome's brows drew together. "Ayden told me you and your brother are close."

I nodded. "We are. Most of the time."

Ayden dropped his arms over the top of the sofa and propped his ankle on his knee. "And then there's the few times when his meddling in Declan's life gets to be too much. Like tonight?"

I looked up at Ayden. "Meddling? I'd take his normal meddling over this bullshit."

"Okay, so what happened? I'm guessing this involves Brock too, otherwise you would have blown up at Ethan tonight and we would have talked tomorrow."

"Brock's the one I'm trying not to blow up on. Ethan's ass is mine tomorrow." I hopped up, my feet carrying me across the floor of their own volition. "Do you know that Brock wasn't supposed to sleep with me? That he promised my brother to keep his hands off?" Ayden and Rome's eyes were so round, I would have laughed if the entire situation wasn't a shitshow. "Yep. Apparently, now my brother has decided he can dictate who I can or cannot date."

Ayden ran his hand through his long, light brown hair. Most of the time he had it up, but tonight, it hung around his shoulders. "That's pushing it, even for him."

"Ya think? I mean, I've known my brother to be overbearing, but this is a whole new level. Then on top of that, Brock didn't bother to tell me any of this. Even when we talked about the right time to tell Ethan about us seeing each other."

"Why didn't you want to tell your brother?" Rome asked.

My shoulders dropped and I took the seat next to Rome again. "Because I figured he'd make Brock jump through hoops first. Like he's done with everyone, from my agent to my batting coach. I had to work hard to get

Brock to let me in and I had no plans on letting Ethan jeopardize that. I wanted to wait until I was sure Brock was all in with me."

Rome laid a small hand on my shoulder. "Sounds like he wants what's best for you."

I sighed. "I know he does. But why would he think his best friend isn't what's best? Out of all the men or women I could be fucking in this world, wouldn't he rather me be with someone he trusts?"

"He should, but Ethan's always looked out for you. I remember him drilling me with questions when we roomed together," Ayden reminded me.

"I know. And while it's way too far, it doesn't completely surprise me. We need to have a talk about boundaries. What I can't believe is that Brock kept it from me. After he promised not to talk to my brother about me, us, anything."

"Did he make that promise before or after his one to Ethan?" Ayden asked.

"It had to be after. Their conversation happened before I moved in. He had the perfect opportunity to bring it up. Instead, he focused on *my* reasons for not wanting to tell my brother yet."

It was silent for a moment. Ayden and Rome shared a look, then Ayden spoke up again. "Look, I get it, Brock and Ethan both fucked up royally here. But that doesn't stop you from loving either one of them, does it?"

"No. It doesn't"

"You know I love you like a brother, man, so I'm gonna lay it all out for you. You need to talk to Brock. I told you last week to tell him how you feel. Yes, he still kept the conversation with Ethan from you, but would you have been able to face Ethan together earlier? Brock's in this as much as you are. I could see it all over his face when he watched you at the barbecue."

"He watched me?"

Rome patted my knee. "Oh, he watched you all night. Didn't matter who you were talking to, he had his eyes only on you. Ayden's right. That man loves you."

I let that process for a moment and looked up at the two of them. "I'm not ready to talk yet. I don't want to say anything I don't mean."

"And you don't have to be ready to talk tonight. Sleep on it and see how you feel in the morning."

Ayden was right. A little more time was exactly what I needed. In the morning light, things wouldn't look so bad, and I'd be able to focus on what I really wanted to say. I stood up and took my keys from my pocket. "Thanks. You knew exactly what to say."

Ayden blew on his fingers and brushed them on his shirt. "I know."

I chuckled and looked down at Rome. "And thank you for letting me interrupt your night."

"Always. We're family."

I turned toward the door when Ayden calling my name stopped me. "You're always welcome to stay the night."

"I know, but tonight I think I should go home. Then I can talk to everyone in the morning."

"That's a good plan." Ayden walked me to the door. "I'll see you tomorrow."

"Night." I waved on my way to the car and climbed inside. The drive home would give me a little more time to think.

The heaviness in my heart hadn't lifted completely when I pulled into the garage, but I felt lighter than I had when I arrived at Ayden's. It was late enough that Brock should be in bed. I could go up to the guest room to sleep off the last bit of anger then Brock and I could talk tomorrow, hopefully before Ethan woke up. If I had my way, we were all going to have a nice long sit-down about secrets, lies, and controlling my life. All of it was coming out in the open, whether they liked it or not.

I shut the engine off and did my best to quietly climb the stairs and go inside. I knew Sampson would hear me come in, no matter what. As long as everyone else stayed asleep. I didn't get a single step through the door when I noticed Brock still sitting on the couch where I'd left him hours earlier.

He turned his head to look at me and stood. I didn't move. Not toward him. Not away. I simply stood there. The mood to talk still hadn't hit me. My love for Brock hadn't changed, which was why I wouldn't talk and end up flinging insults at him.

"Dec, please say something."

"I'm not ready to talk yet."

With that, I moved toward the stairs, taking them up quietly to the guest room where I planned to stay for the rest of the night.

Chapter 28

Brock

Sleep eluded me long after Declan came home and refused to talk to me. It was like he punched me square in the chest when he said he wasn't ready, but what did I expect? That he'd come home and suddenly he'd understand? Everything would be all right? That wasn't going to happen. Declan was angry and rightfully so.

So, I wallowed in my self-induced misery for hours. I had no one to blame for this but myself. Well, I could blame Ethan, but I was the one who made the promise, even though I was angry at him for bringing it up to begin with. I also should have told Declan about it sooner. Right when things started progressing between us. That was solely on me. No way was Ethan going to say something to Declan about it.

I ambled down the stairs after the sun rose, done with staying in my room. Plus, I wanted to see Declan as soon as he woke up. It was so hard not to knock on his door as I passed by. I paused and debated doing it, but in the end decided against it. I wondered if he slept or if he was up all night like I was.

With the coffee starting, I walked over to the sliding door to let Sampson out to take care of business. The slow drip of the coffee helped soothe me a little. Lali told me I should give in and buy a Keurig already, but I liked my coffee the way it was. I didn't want to change it.

Looking out at the small dune and the ocean beyond it, everything seemed so peaceful. So simple. But inside me, my heart was slowly breaking as fear churned my stomach. I had no idea what was going to happen when Declan woke up. All I could do was hope we could get through this.

As I was letting Sampson in, I heard footsteps on the stairs behind me. I hoped it was Declan and not Ethan. I didn't want to see Ethan yet. I had to talk to Declan first. I had to make things right.

Declan didn't look much better than I felt. He had bags under his eyes; he was walking slower than normal. He played hard last night, only to come home and get into an argument with me. What he needed was rest but I couldn't put things off any longer. Now I felt awful for not letting him get a good night's sleep and talking to him this morning.

It took everything in me not to go to him. Not to wrap him in my arms and tell him how sorry I was. Instead, I let Sampson get his morning pets as I closed the sliding door, then I walked over to pull two mugs down for coffee. I worked to get both drinks how we liked them while Declan murmured low to Sampson.

Who knew I'd be jealous over my dog getting more attention from him than I was?

Declan straightened and came over to the counter where I was. I handed him the mug and our fingers lightly brushed. It sent a pang of yearning through me. Would I ever get to hold him again? I wasn't sure how angry he was. He came back here last night, so that had to count for something. He could have stayed out all night and came back to pack his things. He didn't have to stay here but I was happy he did.

We stood staring at one another for a moment, our mugs in hand. Declan nodded toward the couch. I followed behind him just like Sampson was, who decided to hop up on the couch on Declan's other side.

"I can see you're itching to speak, so go ahead," he told me.

It was like I had no control over my mouth as everything poured from me. "I'm so sorry, Dec. I didn't mean to hurt you and that's exactly what I did. I shouldn't have made that promise to Ethan. I knew right when he said it that it was wrong, but I wanted your brother to be happy, just like I always want you to be the same. You're part of my family and I'd do anything for both of you.

"But then you came here, and everything changed. I no longer saw the boy I grew up with or the man I only interacted with on occasion, thanks to our careers getting in the way. I got to know you for who you are now. The kind, caring, loving man in front of me. You're everything, Dec. Everything right in my world. I'm so much happier when you're around. Like nothing bad can touch me when you're near. But it has. It did when I made that promise to Ethan.

"I know there's nothing I can do to take it back. I would if I could. But I wouldn't take back you and me and this relationship we built. I'll do anything to make things right. Whatever you want. And I will never lie to you again."

"You don't get it. The promise is the least of my worries. That's something I need to talk to Ethan about, who should have never asked that of you in the first place. You lied to me. A lie of omission is still a lie."

I scratched along the back of my neck. "I know. I shouldn't have done that. The further we went, the harder it was to tell you what had been said. I thought for sure you'd leave me once it was out in the open. I was so scared. The thought of you not being in my life anymore... it guts me, Dec."

"Fear I understand. I've had plenty of my own when it comes to you. Trust is a two-way street, and I need to know that you'll always be honest with me."

"I haven't lied to you about anything else and I never intend to. I trust you with my life, Dec. Down to my very soul. You have to know you mean the world to me. I'd never intentionally hurt you."

"A part of me knows that. Then there's the part last night that questioned everything else you told me about your conversations with Ethan. If we're going to do this, I need to know that you won't keep things from me."

"I won't. I promise. Never again. This... you... you're who I need and want in my life. You're who matters. I..." I swallowed, trying to get the words out I longed to say. "I love you, Dec. Please tell me I didn't ruin us."

"You didn't. I love you, too, Brock."

"Fuck, I love you so much."

Leaning in, I hesitantly pressed my lips to his. I wasn't sure if I'd ever get to taste him again. If I'd get to feel him like I had. But he was here in front of me, saying I didn't ruin everything by not divulging what was said between Ethan and me. I didn't deserve his forgiveness, but I wasn't stupid enough not to take it.

One of Declan's hands went to my cheek and the other to my chest. He turned his head slightly to deepen the kiss then it was like everything in me was on fire. So much need roared through me. I wanted his clothes off. I wanted him buried inside me. I wanted it all at once.

When I leaned in to take things further, I felt Sampson's wet nose against my hand where it sat on Declan's leg.

Pulling back, I glanced down at my dog. "Seriously? You need to butt in right at this very moment? Did you not get enough attention when Dec woke up?"

Declan chuckled beside me. "He's cockblocking us."

I sighed and leaned back against the couch. "Freaking dog." My stomach took the opportunity to make itself known. I hadn't eaten since the game last night and now that things were okay between Declan and me, my appetite roared back to life. "Since this isn't going any further at the moment, how about some breakfast?"

He smiled and it was absolutely stunning. Declan never ceased to take my breath away. Everything about him was so right for me. "Sure."

I left Declan on the couch and went to the kitchen to start pulling things out. I whipped up scrambled eggs, some turkey sausage, which I knew Declan wasn't a fan of, but it was what we had. I also put some wheat bread in the toaster.

While I was busy cooking, I felt arms slip around my waist a moment before Declan put his chin on my shoulder. I leaned back against him, not taking my eyes off the food so I didn't burn it. "I missed you. I missed this. I'm glad we're okay."

"Me, too."

Sampson perked up all the sudden and walked toward the stairs. Declan pulled away from me and went to sit at the small table with his coffee. A moment later, Ethan entered the room.

"Morning," he said with a smile. "That was the best I've slept in a while."

"Sit," Declan demanded, pointing at the chair across from him.

I plated the food and turned the burners off, knowing if I didn't, I'd forget and it would burn. I quickly turned the oven on to keep everything warm and slipped the food inside.

"We're not gonna have little chats about sleep and happy mornings," Declan started. "We have some things to talk about and you need to listen."

Ethan narrowed his eyes at his brother. I was sure he wanted to say something, but considering the look on Declan's face, I thought Ethan was wise to keep his mouth shut.

Ethan lowered himself into the chair, his gaze never straying from Declan's. While there were things Ethan and I needed to discuss, I was staying out of this part of the conversation.

"What's up?" Ethan could act innocent, but I knew better. Declan had never confronted his brother before and Ethan didn't know what to do.

"What's up is I need you to be my big brother and not my fucking parents. I'm sick and tired of talking to you on the phone, or when you come to visit, about all the good things in my life only to have you turn around and treat me like a child."

"I don't treat—"

"Stop speaking. You can talk once I'm finished. I love you, Ethan. You're my brother and have always looked out for me. But I'm a goddamn adult. You don't have to worry about me paying the bills or doing my laundry. We should be talking about baseball and movies. Not my responsibilities." Declan stood. "And you definitely don't get to decide who I am and who I am not allowed to date." Declan looked over at me and I knew it was my turn.

Here was where my cursing came out. Because fuck me I had to jump in here and defend everything I had with Declan. Make Ethan see we were right for each other.

"I told him." I didn't give Ethan time to say anything before I kept going. "I couldn't keep it from him. It wasn't right that you had me promise to keep my hands off your brother. You shouldn't have done that, and I knew from the start it wasn't right, yet I agreed and I'm at fault for that."

Ethan frowned. "What are you talking about?"

I drew in a deep breath and let it out. "Dec and I, well, we're together."

His eyebrows furrowed. "Together?" He looked from me to Declan then watched as his brother reached over and took my hand in his. "The fuck? When did this happen?"

"Been happening for a while." Declan squeezed my hand. I could deal with Ethan. I got myself into this mess, I had to get myself out, although it was nice knowing I had Declan here with me. He gave me the courage I needed. "We're not just screwing around, Ethan. Dec and I love each other."

"Hold on. You're in love? In the two months since Declan moved here, you fell in love?"

I nodded. "Yeah, and the guilt at making that promise to you has been hanging over my head since it started. You have no idea what that did to me."

"But you said just because you two both liked men that you wouldn't end up in bed together."

"How was I supposed to know what was going to happen? I'm not a fortune teller. I didn't know how easily and fast I'd fall for your brother. But it happened and he's the best thing in my life. I mean it, Ethan, I love him."

Ethan scrubbed his hands over his face then studied us again. "Well, shit." He sat there like he was rolling everything over in his mind. He focused on Declan. "You, too? You're sure you love him?"

Declan rolled his eyes. "I'd think I'd know when I was in love. So yes, I love him."

"I was not expecting this when I came here." He chuckled but it wasn't completely with humor. It sounded a little pained and a little uneasy. "I'm not sure what to say."

"Say you're not going to stand in our way," I told him. "You don't have to say you're happy for us. I'm not sure I'd expect that. But we won't be hiding this any longer."

Declan gently tugged on my hand. I peered over at him. "What are you saying?"

"No more hiding, Dec. I'm going to call my parents after breakfast and tell them everything. Next time you and I leave this house, it will be with my hand in yours. I want everyone to know about us."

"Brock..."

I leaned over until my lips were only a breath from his. "I love you, Dec."

Instead of saying the words back, he closed the distance between us to show me how much he loved me, too.

"All right, that's enough," Ethan cut in. His voice drew Declan and me apart. "I won't stand in your way, but I'm sure as hell not going to sit here while you two make out." There was a thundercloud of emotions playing across his face.

Releasing Declan's hand, I leaned closer to Ethan and gripped his shoulder. "You know I love you, too, right? You've always been as much a brother to me, same as Wyatt has."

"Doesn't that make what you and Declan are doing a little—"

"No! What's wrong with you?"

"What's wrong with me? You're sleeping with my brother! I need food to fully wrap my head around this."

"Fine, let me grab it from the oven."

No, I didn't think everything would be perfect with Ethan, but he knew about Declan and me. What he did going forward was on him. I, for one, was happy and couldn't wait to share that with the rest of my family.

Chapter 29

Declan

The bright morning sun burning through my eyelids reminded me whose bed I crawled into the night before. Only Brock could sleep with the shades wide open and not be annoyed at the early hour wake-up call. I snuggled farther into his warmth. The air conditioner keeping my skin above the blanket cool.

The night before, it seemed like a simple decision to climb into bed with Brock after the game. When I'd had to leave for the stadium, there was still an underlying tension between Ethan and Brock, even with Ethan and me. Ethan wasn't being outright hostile, but there was still a change in his demeanor. One I hoped would go away with the more time that passed. Brock had been on such a roll that I didn't want to stop him to point out to Ethan that I'd loved Brock in some way, shape, or form for years. Falling in love with him hadn't taken much more.

I knew I needed to explain to Ethan. Make him see exactly why Brock and I together were perfect. Anything to knock down the last barrier to accepting us as a couple. Unfortunately, by the time I got home everyone had been asleep. That was the moment I decided there was nowhere else I was sleeping but in Brock's arms.

Now that I was here with his clean scent invading my senses, I could no longer deny my body's reaction as my morning wood turned into a lust driven hard-on. I leaned back and dug in the table behind me and grabbed the bottle of lube and a condom. Placing them both within reach, I snuggled up to Brock's back once again. This time my hand found its way over his hip. The back of my fingers grazed along his own morning erection.

Soft snores still filled the space. I figured I'd love waking up with Brock's hand wrapped around my dick and didn't he deserve the same? I took hold of Brock and with slow movements, slid my hand up and down his shaft. Those soft snores turned into heavy breathing over time.

"Fuck—" I slapped my hand over Brock's mouth.

"No, no, no. I don't need Ethan busting in here or freaking out on us later." I didn't stop the movement of my hand as I bit down lightly on his lobe. "Now, you're gonna be quiet while I make you feel like screaming my name."

Brock nodded and I kept stroking him. Like satiny silk beneath my fingertips, I moved my hand up and down, stopping every so often to swipe my thumb around the tip to spread his precum around. Brock didn't make another sound as he thrust his hips forward into the tight grip of my fist.

"Please. More," he whispered so low I almost didn't hear him.

He whined slightly when I took my hand from his shaft. "Soon enough. Be patient."

I popped open the lube and spread some across my fingers, sliding them between his cheeks to his tight pucker. He opened easily for my first finger, and it wasn't long before I had two fingers sliding in and out of him. Brock shoved his hips back, chasing my fingers as they retreated from his body.

I slid a third finger in but knew Brock wouldn't last long with the way he was gripping his shaft. Letting my fingers slip free, I rolled on the condom and coated up my cock. I grazed my fingers over his thigh and pushed his leg forward, opening Brock even farther so I could slip my dick inside.

A loud moan started, but Brock slammed his own hand over his mouth while I buried myself to the hilt. Our bodies moved in tandem as we both reached for the climax in sight. The sound of slapping skin filled the room with me taking Brock and myself to new heights. It wasn't long before his body tightened its grasp on mine to the point I thought I might pass out. I couldn't hold on any longer and released into the condom.

As we came down from our orgasms, I leaned forward and nibbled on his lobe. "This week we're getting tested and the next time I take you, I'm coming inside you." His hole spasmed around me a bit more.

"If I hadn't already come hard enough to melt my brain cells, I would have come again."

"I think I like the sound of that. We'll have to test your stamina one of these nights."

Brock groaned low in his throat. "You're killing me."

I slipped from Brock's body and missed the tight heat almost immediately. The benefit was it wouldn't be the last time I felt it.

Knowing Ethan would be up soon, if he wasn't already, I moved toward the edge of the bed. "I'm going to go get in the shower before my brother gets out of bed. I love that he knows we're together, but there's no need to rub it in his face."

Brock rolled to his other side and propped his head on his arm. "I could join you."

I laughed and backed my way toward the bathroom. "Not unless you want Ethan barging in here. I'm pretty sure we just tested the limits of your ability to be quiet. I'm not sure you can do it again."

A smirk lifted the corner of his mouth. "Probably not. You feel way too good inside me."

It was my turn to groan as I shut the bathroom door. I had to get away from Brock's tempting body before I climbed back in bed with him and did something that would get us both in trouble.

I raced through my shower then headed downstairs, leaving Brock in bed. The minute I hit the bottom floor, Sampson greeted me and ran to the back door. I let him out and stood on the deck, inhaling the warm, salty air.

It was perfect for a beach day, that was if Ethan still wanted to go. I hadn't talked to my brother since I'd left the weird, awkward silence the day before to go to the stadium.

I heard the screen door open but didn't bother turning around. I knew Brock would join me as soon as he finished his shower.

"Hiding from me?"

That was not the voice I expected. I glanced to my left to see Ethan moving forward to stand next to me at the railing. He didn't look upset, at least not on the outside. I could see the tension lining each of his muscles in his arms.

"Nope, letting Sampson out while Brock's in the shower." He didn't say anything else, simply laid his arms on the railing and looked straight out into the ocean. I couldn't let this strange tension continue. My brother may be overbearing at times, but he was still my brother. We'd always been close, and I refused to let my relationship with Brock ruin it. "Want to tell me why it pisses you off that I'm dating him?"

"You're not just dating him."

I almost sputtered at the bluntness in Ethan's response. "No, I'm not. That's not a reason you should be pissed off for, though. I'd be sleeping with anyone I dated. So, I'll ask again, why does it piss you off that I'm dating Brock?"

"Because he promised me he wouldn't go near you."

The anger started bubbling up and I shoved it back down. The time for yelling ended yesterday. If the relationship between me and Brock was ever going to be okay in the eyes of my brother, we had to address the elephant in the room.

I stood up and turned to face him. "I don't think that's it either. If I were to guess, I'd say there would never be anyone good enough for me in your eyes." His jaw tightened and I knew I hit the right mark, so I pushed forward. "You've always looked out for me, keeping me from making mistakes that have saved me some serious heartache and bullshit. I know you're doing the same now. You don't want me to get hurt." I took a step toward him and laid my hand on his shoulder. "You're my brother and I love you. I love that you don't want me to get hurt, but that's not going to happen this time."

He finally looked away from the horizon and up at me. "You don't know that. Anybody can hurt you."

"You're right. Anyone can. But shouldn't that be one of those life lessons I need to learn on my own? You can't bulldoze every obstacle in my path. There are times that I'm going to have to get hurt and learn from it. *This* isn't one of those."

"How can you be so sure?"

I pulled my hand back and crossed my arms over my chest. "Do you have so little trust in your best friend that you'd think he'd hurt me?"

"That's not what I'm—"

I cut him off, knowing his excuse was complete bullshit. "That's exactly what you're saying. Brock, a man you have trusted your entire life, shared every secret with, every problem, isn't trustworthy of protecting the heart of your little brother. That he's not good enough for me."

Ethan was silent, his gaze moving back over the water. Hopefully, my words were hitting their mark. I wanted Ethan to see how he was treating Brock, the man he called his best friend, but also how he was treating me. Like he couldn't trust me to make smart decisions for myself.

The tension grew between us when Ethan finally turned to me. "You're right. I'm sorry." I stood stock-still, not expecting Ethan to give in that quickly. I thought I'd have to argue a little longer about why Brock and me together were perfect. Ethan chuckled. "You look like you don't know what to say."

"That's 'cause I don't. I thought I'd have to keep arguing for a little bit."

Ethan sighed. "I've always looked out for you and you're right when you say I wouldn't trust anyone with your heart, but if I have to trust someone, Brock is the perfect person. I trust him with my life, which means I can trust him with yours."

I reached out, grabbed Ethan's hand, and yanked him into a hug. Over his shoulder, I could see Brock standing in the living room watching the two of us. He mouthed, "Okay?" I sent him a thumbs-up and patted my brother on the back before letting him go.

I cupped my hand over his shoulder and guided him to the door. "Now, let's go see what Brock is making for breakfast. I'm starving."

"You're always hungry." Ethan chuckled.

"Yes, but once we eat, we can go to the beach without you listening to me bitch about it. Pancakes and apologies sound great together." Ethan elbowed me in the side and laughed even harder as we stepped back into the house, Sampson following quickly on our heels.

After a breakfast of turkey sausage omelets and fruit salad, we changed and started down to the beach. When we reached the edge of Brock's property, I took his hand in mine and we walked down to the water together. As we crested over the dunes, I noticed Reed walking back toward his own house. His mouth dropped open when he saw Brock holding my hand. I waved as we walked by. I'd seen him attempt to hit on Brock, but I could see how uncomfortable it made Brock. Hopefully, now it would stop, and we could all be friends. Reed was a nice guy.

I didn't care how many people were down here or how many more people gave us the shocked looks we got from Reed, I wanted the world to finally know that this man was mine. And what better way for that to happen than a day at the beach with my love and my brother.

Chapter 30

Brock

It had been two weeks since everything happened with Ethan. Since then, it felt like so much had changed, but at the same time, so much was the same.

I came out to my parents, which was more nerve-wracking than it needed to be. I knew they'd accept me and be supportive, but that didn't mean I wasn't nervous telling them. While I was on video chat with them, Wyatt was there and came out as well. I was glad we got to share the moment. I only wished I would have been there in person to get hugs from my parents like Wyatt did. That was okay, though. I'd see them the next time I went to visit, and I was sure they'd hug me within an inch of my life when I did.

Declan and I were doing amazing together. We didn't hide our relationship. All it took was us on the beach that day with Ethan before someone took a photo of us and posted it on social media. I didn't mind at all.

And Lali put out a statement on behalf of the Sandpipers after it happened saying how proud the team was of me and how they'd always have my back. I wasn't naïve enough to think everyone on the team would be supportive; however, I didn't need them to be. Those who mattered to me were.

Out on my deck, I was enjoying my morning coffee while Sampson pushed around one of his toys in the sand below. Declan left not long ago for the road. He'd only be gone a few days, but I still hated to see him leave. I had to keep my eye on the prize—the end of the season. Then I'd get to wake up every morning with Declan.

One more month and I'd be starting college for the second time. It was going to be a lot of hard work, but I was doing it for my future. With Declan by my side, I knew anything was possible and he'd be there with me for the journey. He had years left to play ball. I needed to do something with my life besides sit around the house. It wasn't about the money. I had more than I needed. It was about being something other than a football player. Being what I dreamed of.

Wyatt and I talked over the phone about possibly joining forces and doing something together once I graduated with my master's. Until then, he got a job that he'd start in a few weeks. He was going to gain experience while I furthered my education.

"Oh my god! It's Brock Richmond! And have you heard? He's gay and shacking up with one of the Espen Emperors!" I'd know that voice anywhere.

I stood with a huge grin and peered over the railing to find my brother standing there with a matching smile. Sampson bolted over to the side of the fence to greet him as well. He didn't see Wyatt often, but he never forgot him.

"Get up here, kid!" I called down.

"I gotta get my bags out of the car."

"We'll get them in a minute. Come up here first."

Wyatt reached over to the gate and unlatched it so he could come inside. Sampson was on him immediately. He wasn't a jumper normally, but he pushed right up to put his paws on Wyatt's chest, almost knocking him down. Wyatt chuckled while he gave Sampson love. It was obvious my brother missed him just as much.

We never had any pets growing up. We couldn't afford them. Then Wyatt went away to college and my parents didn't have the urge for a furry companion. But Wyatt... I had a feeling one day he'd have his own dog or cat or maybe both.

Eventually, Sampson got down and both of them came up the stairs to the deck. I immediately wrapped my brother in a hug. He was shorter than me by five inches. Me being broader than him allowed me to fully engulf him, until he patted my arm so I could release him for some much-needed breathing space.

I put my hands on his shoulders to get a good look at him. Video chat just wasn't the same as having the person right in front of me.

Wyatt's eyes, which were the same dark brown as mine, gleamed in the morning sunlight. His hair matched his eyes in color and was tousled like he drove the whole way here in the summer heat with the windows down. His hair was getting longer, falling over his ears in soft waves. He looked great.

"How was the drive?" I asked.

"Good. Coming out here on a Monday was smart. I missed the weekend rush to the beach."

"I'm glad. Let's get your stuff then have some breakfast. I have a quiche in the oven."

"You didn't have to cook for me, Brock. We could have gone out to eat on me."

I ruffled his hair. He quickly ducked away then swatted at me. He hated when I did that. "Nah, I like to cook. You know that. Besides, I was up for a while this morning and needed something to do. Dinner tonight is out with Lali. Once she heard you were coming to town, she wanted to see you."

"I do love her. Too bad you aren't attracted to women. She'd be a hell of a catch."

"We'd never work as anything other than friends."

"For many reasons."

I laughed. "True."

We went down to his car to bring his bags in. He had his laptop with him. It wasn't smart to leave it in the car in the heat. Back inside, Wyatt took a couple glasses out of the cabinet and poured juice while I took the quiche out of the oven. I cut it and plated it before bringing it over to the table. Wyatt made himself a cup of coffee as well, then took a seat.

He grinned when he saw the food. "You're the best brother."

"You're only saying that because I made this for you."

"Well, yeah. You put bacon and ham in here, a few different cheeses by the looks of it, and left out the healthy stuff I eat every day. That's how I know you love me. You spoil me with food I shouldn't be having."

"Only for you." I loved to indulge my brother and cooking was a great way for me to do it.

"How's Dec doing?"

"Good. He's playing out in Philly for a few days then he'll be back. He's excited to see you. Been a while."

"It has. It will be nice to spend some time with him again."

"I bet it will be good to be away from Mom and Dad, too."

He groaned. "You know I love them, Brock, but I have zero time to myself when I'm there. I can't wait to start working so I can save up for an apartment. I need out. The other night, I left for a hookup and Mom kept asking where I was going and who I was going to see. I lied and said it was a date. Dad rushed away then came back and handed me condoms and a travel-sized bottle of lube. I get that they're trying to be supportive, but eww."

I cringed then laughed, mostly because it happened to him and not me. I would have turned bright red if Dad had done that to me. "I'm sorry. Want to borrow some money to get out faster?" I would just give it to him if he wanted it, but Wyatt made it clear that I was only allowed to pay for his college and nothing else. What I really wanted to do was buy him a more reliable car. The twenty-year-old Honda Accord he drove had seen better days. It was my mom's, who gave it to him when he went away to college. Mom always loved getting rides to and from work with Dad.

"What did you say to Dad when he handed that to you?"

"Say?" he asked with his voice slightly higher pitched. "I couldn't say anything. I took what he offered and bolted out the door so fast I was surprised the soles of my sneakers didn't melt off. I wasted time the next morning at a cafe until they were both at work before I went back to the house."

"Then evening rolled around, and they came home..."

"And I got asked more questions, including if the lube was good. Dad said he wanted to make sure I had quality... products."

I couldn't help it. I barked out a laugh. "Is that why you changed from staying here from one week to two?"

"You can kick me out at any time. I'll stay at a hotel. I just had to get out of there. I know you and Dec like your alone time."

"Are you kidding? You're welcome here for as long as you'd like to stay. Besides, Dec has to travel again next week for even longer. I'll love having the company."

"Only if you're sure."

"I wouldn't have invited you if I wasn't."

After breakfast, we cleaned up then Wyatt got settled in the spare bedroom—the room Declan stayed in when he first got here. We'd since moved Declan's things out of that room and into mine, or ours, as it were now.

Declan and I had a long talk about living arrangements. I fully supported him still buying a home in Espen, even though it made my chest tight to think of him leaving here. This place felt so much more like a home with him here. Or maybe it was just Declan. He was my home.

I smiled thinking about part of the conversation.

"You can stay here longer, Dec. Or forever. Whichever is best for you."

He smiled from where he sat, straddling my waist in bed. "Is this your way of asking me to move in with you?"

"You already live here, but yeah, I... I want you here. I don't want you to go anywhere else." If the lights in the room had been on, I knew my blush would have been visible.

Declan leaned down and pressed his lips to mine. He moved after a heated kiss, so his face was tucked against my neck. "I love it here, Brock. I don't want to be anywhere else."

And just like that, Declan and I agreed to live together, permanently. Just yesterday he got an offer on his home down in Maryland. He accepted and the paperwork had been started to sell it. He even started moving some of his stuff in, including his favorite chair, which was now in the living room.

With the happy memory on my mind, I changed into a pair of swim shorts and a T-shirt then slathered on sunblock. Wyatt wanted to go down to the beach. I was surprised he waited this long. He'd probably spend more time in the water than he did with me, but that was okay. I loved seeing my brother happy and swimming in the ocean did that.

When I got to the bottom of the stairs with my beach towel in hand, Wyatt was there waiting for me, practically bouncing on the balls of his feet.

"Ready?" he asked.

"Yeah, just let me grab my phone." I already had my house key clipped to my shorts so I wouldn't lose it or have to carry it.

I gave Sampson a pat on the head then made sure he had plenty of water. We said goodbye to him with a promise to walk him on the beach later tonight when it was quiet.

We weren't on the beach for a full minute before I heard my name being called. I glanced over to find Reed waving to me. His friends were around him, although he left them to come over to us. The closer he got, I realized his eyes left me and went right for Wyatt.

"Hello, Wyatt." He gave him a bright smile. "I haven't seen you in a while."

I glanced over at my brother to find him raking his eyes over Reed in interest. "The last time I was here we didn't get to see each other."

"You two are welcome to join us. We're just brainstorming for our gym."

"On the beach?" I asked.

"We don't need a conference room for these conversations. There's no better backdrop than the ocean."

I shook my head and smiled. "Whatever you say."

"Brock, will you hold my towel?" Wyatt asked. "I want to..." He hooked his thumb over his shoulder at the ocean.

"Sure." I took his towel and Wyatt made a slow jog out to the water then dove right in.

"Your brother's looking good, Brock," Reed said, bringing my eyes back to him. "How long is he here for?"

"A couple weeks. Listen, Reed—"

He held up his hand. "I won't go breaking his heart or anything, if that's what you're worried about. There's nothing wrong with a summer fling. Wait." His eyes widened. "He's gay, right, or bi? The way he was looking at me, I figured he was."

"He's gay." Wyatt didn't care who knew about him since he came out to our parents.

"Good." His gaze went back out to the ocean, where my brother was swimming farther out to sea.

Wyatt was a grown man and if he wanted to get involved with Reed, that was up to him. I knew Reed was a good guy. There were way worse out there for Wyatt to hook up with, even if it was only for a couple weeks. Plus, it was nice to see Reed showing interest in Wyatt instead of me. At least my dad wouldn't be here passing out condoms and lube.

I visibly shook the thought away. I really wished Wyatt hadn't told me that.

Chapter 31

Declan

Two months later.

Strike.

Bottom of the sixth inning, we were up three games in the World Series. If you would have asked me a year ago, I never would have imagined being here, playing in this game. I loved my time with the Backfins. The team and players were great, but it took a team like the Emperors to make it to the final game.

Ayden was on the mound. With all the talk about last year's League Championship Series, I knew the team was worried how he would react being the starter for game five. In some ironic twist of fate, Ayden had ended up on the mound in the same game he'd lost the year before. Even though I'd talked to him after the loss, I hadn't realized the depth of the impact it had on him at the time. The difference this year was the fact that this time it was the World Series, and it was three to one with us in the lead, not the other way around.

The ball came back from Marcus into Ayden's glove, and I watched as he settled himself, readying for the next pitch. He had the same routine each time he pitched. Even as my heart raced faster with each inning, we made it through still up by two runs, it gave me a sense of comfort watching him adjust his stance on the mound.

Strike.

I glanced up to the boxes where our loved ones waited. My parents, Ethan, and Brock. That was another thing I never could have envisioned for myself. The crush of my teenage years—the love of my life—waiting with my family, sharing this moment with me. If we won, it would be the first World Series of my career. Hopefully, not the last either.

I knew Brock's eyes were trained on me as I stood ready in right field, waiting for the ball a batter might hit. With the way Ayden was pitching, that would only be an extreme circumstance. Each batter who had come up against him hadn't gotten more than a small piece of the ball. Most of the hits going to the infield.

Strike.

The last out of the top of the sixth, I jogged to the dugout. Having bat in the last inning, I dropped down onto the bench and grabbed a bottle of water. Butterflies took flight in my stomach. A few more runs and hits in this inning could seal the deal on this series and make the Emperors World Series Champions once again.

Ayden sat down next to me. "How you holding up out there?"

I shrugged. "Pretty slow night. The pitcher keeps striking 'em out. Think you have a few more innings in you?"

Ayden lifted his arm and rolled his shoulder a few times. "I might."

The crack of a ball hitting wood drew our attention to the field. We raced to the railing in time to see Vander's ball fly high into the outfield, over the heads of the fielders, and into the seats of the sold-out home crowd.

"Fuck yeah!" I yelled.

The stadium erupted almost as much as the dugout. A single home run widened our lead. We met Vander as he crossed home plate. High fives and cheers were shared, but the game wasn't over. We had to go back to work. Dominic grounded out, followed by a strikeout by Olivera, the center fielder. Callen's turn up to bat hadn't brought in anymore runs. Back on the field we went.

The next two innings had the batters from both teams going down in order. The top of the ninth and this was our last chance to blow the lead we had. Joe had pulled Ayden after the seventh inning. The speed on his fast ball slowing, you could see the exhaustion in his entire body after each pitch. The Emperors' closer, Dave Meller, was on the mound looking for the last three outs of the Series.

Sure, if we lost tonight, we could come back tomorrow for another shot. It would be a win, not the sweet vindication Ayden needed after the last year's League Championship. He'd worked his ass off tonight to keep their team off the bases, and we'd put in the work to get the runs to pull us ahead. Now it came down to three outs to end the game.

The first batter came to the plate. One, two, three, down he went. Same for the second batter. Tingles raced along my skin as the third batter in the lineup stepped up to hit. Strike one went flying over the plate at over a hundred miles an hour. The second strike just as fast. This was it. The end of the game. Dave wound up and let go. I waited to hear the satisfying smack of the ball as it hit Marcus's glove. I saw the swing and heard it connect at the same time I saw the ball flying past Callen and into left field.

Vander raced after it, getting the ball back to Callen, keeping the guy on first. My stomach tightened a bit. That was not what I had expected. Neither was the next guy up getting walked. The tying run was up to bat.

Strike.

I breathed a little easier. Pitch two that same distinguishable crack hit my ears. The ball came sailing through first and second toward me. I bolted forward and scooped up the ball, getting back to Dave before a run could score.

Bases loaded. Two outs and the go ahead run up to bat. If it came down to it, we still had half an inning to win the game. I wanted to win at home. In Espen. If we lost tonight, we were heading down to Florida to finish the series. No home field advantage. No home crowds cheering for us.

No, I wanted to win this game tonight.

Marcus stood and pushed his mask up, walking to the mound. The rest of the infield followed. Dave needed a pep talk. It wasn't often he got himself into situations like this. Most of the time he could get himself out. Not always, though. I moved back into right and looked over at Jose Olivera. I could see the same anxious nerves reflected on his face.

The home plate ump stepped out toward the mound and the team dispersed back to their positions. Dave rolled his shoulders a few times, moving his head back and forth like he was cracking his neck. He readied the pitch. My entire body felt like a live wire, ready to light at any moment. Every muscle tense and on alert. The ball went sailing over the plate, right into Marcus's glove. Two more to go.

Dave's second pitch didn't seem to have the same speed on it. Bat connected with ball, high into the air, right into center field. Jose ran forward, waving Vander and me off as he settled under the ball.

Smack.

The crowd erupted as the umpire called the final out. I didn't bother listening as I ran toward Jose. Vander and I reached him first, tackling him to the ground. Bodies piled on top of us, one by one. All giving Jose a good smack on the back.

I was a fucking World Champion.

Holy shit.

I couldn't believe the moment every baseball player wanted in their career had finally come to mine. It was everything I dreamed of and more.

Slowly the pile moved until we were all standing again, and we worked our way back to the middle of the field, where Joe and the rest of the coaches were waiting to share in the celebrations. Coolers were dumped on heads, and everyone was soaked.

"Feels pretty good, doesn't it?" Ayden asked, standing next to me, his long hair no longer pulled back. It was dripping wet.

"It feels fucking fantastic. Seems you shook off that game five issue."

"There was no way I was letting this game end the way that one did."

"You didn't disappoint, man."

He clasped me on the shoulder. "Thanks. And now I'm going to go celebrate with my husband. I'll see you later at the party."

Tim had one of the hotel ballrooms in town reserved to celebrate should we win tonight. I glanced to the right as Ayden walked away to where Rome and his dad stood waiting, to see Brock standing there, a wide smile on his face. The cameras flashed all around us, but that didn't stop me from going over to him and wrapping my arms around him. Our lips met. In the middle of the field surrounded by teammates, coaches, reporters, and families, I lost myself to Brock's kiss. The world around us could have disappeared for all I cared.

A throat clearing next to us had me pulling back and looking over my shoulder to see Ethan standing there, with his arms crossed over his chest and a frown on his face. I lifted my brow and waited. Ethan's frown morphed into a smile.

"Congratulations." Ethan wrapped me up in a hug, patting me on the back.

"Thanks." I looked around at the celebrations happening in every direction. "This is more than I could have imagined.

"We're so proud of you," my mom said, pulling me from my brother's arms. My dad came next, then I found my way back to Brock's side. I loved my parents, but celebrating with the man beside me made everything that much better.

"Are you guys coming to the party?"

Mom shook her head. "No. It's been a few long, nerve-wracking days. I'm ready for bed." Dad slipped his hand in to hers. "But I would love to have breakfast—" Her eyes roamed over my teammates "—make that lunch tomorrow before we head home."

Brock leaned forward and pressed a kiss to my mom's cheek. "I'll make sure he's out of bed and ready to go."

Mom laid her hand on his cheek. "Always such a good boy." My parents waved as they went in the direction of the exit.

"I'll be there," Ethan said. "I want to be able to say that I partied with the World Series Champions when I go back to work."

I rolled my eyes. "You can ride over with Brock."

Ethan's eyes darted between me and Brock. "I'll wait in the car."

Ethan walked in the same direction as my parents and the other families that seemed to be on their way out, whether they were headed home or to the party. I turned to Brock and walked straight into his arms.

"You know tonight wouldn't mean as much without you here."

He pressed a kiss to my temple. "I wouldn't have been anywhere else. You were amazing tonight."

"That's 'cause I knew you'd be watching."

Brock lifted his hand and caressed my cheek with his thumb. "I will watch every single game you play until you don't want to play anymore."

I turned my head and kissed his palm. "I'll hold you to that." I leaned forward to whisper in his ear so no one else around us could hear. "And tonight, after we get home, I'm going to lick every inch of your body before I slide deep inside you."

Brock groaned. "And *I'll* hold you to *that*."

Out of the corner of my eye, I noticed the players heading toward the dugout. "Looks like I have to go. I'll see you at the party."

"Definitely." Brock gave me a quick kiss on the lips.

I jogged in the direction of the dugout, noticing I was one of the last still on the field, and waved at Brock as I descended the stairs.

Being traded to Espen had brought more good into my life than I could have imagined. Brock. A life by the beach. And now a World Series Championship. I wasn't sure life could get any better, but I was more than ready to find out.

Epilogue

Brock

Nineteen months later.

When I graduated with my bachelor's degree, I didn't know if I'd ever make it back to Espen University to get my master's. I hoped maybe one day I could. Wished. And here I was. I had graduated with my master's degree in psychology. I felt like the world was opening up to me again. The possibilities were endless.

After the ceremony, I made my way through small clusters of families until I found mine. Not only were my parents and Wyatt there, but Declan was as well. I wasn't sure if he was going to make it. The Emperors had a day game today that went into extra innings. I kept checking my phone on the sly during the ceremony. I wouldn't have blamed him if he couldn't have been here. We knew it was a possibility. But he was and my smile couldn't get any bigger at seeing him.

My mom came to me first and wrapped her arms around me. "Brock..." Her voice was thick with emotion. "I'm so proud of you. I know I've told you that many times over the years but this... today... Your dad and I couldn't be happier."

Pulling back, I peered down at her. Mom was barely five foot five, a solid foot shorter than I was. Tears shimmered in her eyes. "Thanks, Mom. I couldn't have done it without your support." I lifted my head and looked at my dad, Wyatt, and Declan. "All of yours."

Dad came over to hug me next. then Wyatt. Finally, I got my arms around the man I loved more than life itself. "I'm so glad you got here in time."

Dec smiled before leaning in to kiss me. "I told you I'd make it."

I couldn't say anything, too emotional in the moment. So, I simply hugged and kissed him again.

After a bunch of pictures, my parents and Wyatt got into their car, and I followed Declan to his. Inside, we shared more kisses. I was so happy. On top of getting my degree, Declan and I were to be married next year. We'd been engaged for a while but didn't want to plan anything until I was through with college. He had said that was where he wanted my focus. Not that I'd have a lot of time now since I already had the wheels in motion to open a practice with Wyatt, but it was doable with both Declan and me working on the wedding arrangements.

We drove through the city but instead of going back toward our home at the beach, Declan pulled up to a restaurant we knew all too well—Reese's.

"We wanted to take you out to celebrate," he said with a shrug of his shoulders as he parked like it was no big deal.

"You didn't have to do that."

"I know, but we wanted to. You deserve it."

Declan was so good to me. Treated me wonderfully and I did the same with him. I never knew life could be like this. That I could be this happy. And just when I thought I couldn't have a better life, Declan did something to show me how we were only beginning. How this life of ours was wide open.

We went into the restaurant and for a moment, I thought maybe the power was out since the room was bathed in darkness, but then the lights flipped on and shouts of "Surprise!" rang out around us.

The main dining room was filled with our friends and families. My parents were at the front with Wyatt. Beside them I noticed Ethan and his parents. I felt bad not being able to invite them to the graduation. I only got a limited number of tickets. Plus, Ethan had a hard time taking off from work.

"Ethan?" I asked in shock.

He smiled. "Declan wanted it to be a surprise."

I glanced at the man I loved down to my very soul. "You did this?" He nodded. Even though I'd already hugged him and kissed him repeatedly, I embraced him tightly again. "Thank you so much." I was choked up. "Fuck, I love you."

Declan chuckled against me. "I always know when you're emotional because you curse."

After giving him a quick kiss on the lips, I hugged Ethan and his parents.

A throat clearing behind me had my head whipping around. Lali was standing there with her husband, Royce, by her side. "What?" she asked full of faux attitude with her hands on her hips. "Did you think I'd miss this?"

I gaped at her. "I thought you were on your honeymoon."

"I only told you we'd be gone a few more days. We never planned to be away that long. I had to make it back in time to celebrate my best friend graduating college."

"My best friend," Ethan cut in.

Declan's arm around my waist held me tight. "Mine." He grinned, his eyes meeting mine, not at all possessive but completely in love.

"Holy shit," I muttered and quickly wiped away the tears that started to fall from my eyes.

As I looked around at everyone in the room, I noticed a bunch of the Sandpipers' players as well as the guys on the Emperors I'd become close with and their partners. I was floored that everyone had come out to spend this day with me.

"I can't believe you all came."

Kasper Warnes-Wilder stepped up and clasped me on the shoulder. "Since you and Declan got together, you've become part of our family. You've been there for us in one way or another. There is no place we'd rather be than here to celebrate this moment with you. You might not think this warranted a party of this size, but like you've already witnessed, we don't do things in small measures."

I chuckled. These men led busy lives where they traveled a lot, worked hard, and played harder. Kasper was right. This was very fitting. "Well, thank you for coming. It means the world to me."

"Always, Brock."

With that, Kasper turned and gave others a chance to come up and congratulate me. My head was spinning by the time I had a plate full of food and was seated between Wyatt and Declan.

Glancing around the room at those around me, I couldn't believe how many people I had in my corner. And not ones who were superficial. These people were here for me regardless of the situation. Ones who were there when I came out publicly. Who supported me and had our backs when fans started saying stuff online about Declan and me. They were there for the good and the bad. To lift us up, celebrate as they were now, and just be wonderful friends.

I never would have thought the day Declan moved in with me would have changed my life. Not only did he become the single most important person to me, but with him came this network of people I was fortunate to call my family. If only I could go back and tell the younger version of myself what kind of man he'd become. How after all his struggles and secrets he got to have everything he ever wanted.

I was constantly in awe of what I had, of who I had beside me. I never took it for granted. One day I was going to marry Declan Armitage. I was going to stand in front of the very people in this room and vow my life to him. Our future was bright, but our love was brighter.

***

Stay tuned for the final book in the Espen Emperors series, Merry MVP. The guys are back together for Callen and Spencer's wedding. You'll get chapters from all your favorite characters. There will be tears of joy, lots of laughter, and plenty of love.

Sign up for our mailing list and get an EXCLUSIVE BONUS SCENE of Declan and Brock Newsletter Sign-Up: https://bit.ly/2ZGVCyj

Want to hang out with us on Facebook? Join our Reader Group: Haven Hadley's Heroes

Other Books by Haven Hadley

About the Authors

Haven Hadley is romance writing duo Rebecca Brooke and Michelle Dare. After being friends for years, they decided to venture together into the genre they both loved to read—M/M. Slow burn, sexy, angst-filled stories are their favorite. Both are wives and moms who love dogs, the beach, and baseball, even if they root for rival teams. With every Haven Hadley book, you'll get stories filled with emotion, romance, hot scenes, and a happily ever after.

https://havenhadleybooks.com/

Made in United States
North Haven, CT
27 June 2022